paige press

CHARADE BOOK ONE

THE
LIE

STELLA GRAY

Paige Press
Leander, TX 78641

Ebook:
ISBN: 978-1-953520-16-6

Print:
ISBN: 978-1-953520-17-3

ABOUT THIS BOOK

I've been to a million parties with my crush, but he's never acted on it til now.

Ford Malone could have any woman in Chicago, so why fake a relationship with me?

The world knows him as the heir to a real estate fortune, but to me he'll always be my best friend, the man who saved me from my bullies as a boy.

I'm as surprised as anyone when he announces our engagement, but I'll play along.

Nothing has to change except the way we behave--the way we touch--in public.

But his private touches change everything.

Soon the crush I've hidden for so long is threatening to swallow me whole.

If I tell him how I feel, it could ruin our friendship forever.

But if I don't, it might just ruin me.

How many lies can we tell each other before our truth is buried for good?

Book One in the Charade Series.

PROLOGUE

EMZEE

I t's funny how some things can change...but others? They only ever stay the same.

And sometimes, something that looks exactly the same as it always has from the outside can turn out to be *completely* different on the inside.

Like when your favorite French fusion restaurant on the North Side suddenly revamps its entire menu out of nowhere (even though it was already literal perfection). Or when you find out your scary-tough—but financially indulgent—workaholic father is actually a shady-as-hell international criminal. Or when the modeling agency you do photography work for decides to wholly switch up the way they operate, thanks to the arrest and removal of said father/international criminal as CEO, yet the media still wants to paint the place as an evil sex trafficking empire because they have no idea what's really going on behind closed doors.

You know. Just as an example.

The sign in the lobby was brand new, and so was our management team, but beyond that, the offices on the

1

twenty-ninth floor looked basically the same. My brothers and I had stopped doing business under the name KZ Modeling over a year ago. Henceforth, we relaunched as Danica Rose Management, named after our late mother. Getting a new sign made was easy—everything else, everything on the inside, well, that was a lot harder.

Still, I liked the familiar comfort I felt when I walked through the lobby of the fancy high-rise we worked out of. The way it felt the same as it did when I was a kid.

I used to love visiting my father at work when I was younger. Everything was so exciting back then. Back when I was too little, too naïve, too sheltered to know the ugly truth behind the agency's astronomical wealth and success.

It was still crazy to me how oblivious I had been to things that now seemed so utterly obvious. And it was hard not to be angry about all the secrets everyone had kept from me. Not just my father, but my two older brothers as well. They hadn't taken part in the crimes, but they'd known about the whole thing long enough to join forces with the feds in order to take KZM down and get our dad thrown in jail. Meanwhile, I'd been left totally in the dark.

The ensuing trial had been lengthy, public, and very ugly. Stefan and Luka had both testified. After being found guilty on about a million felony charges, our dad was sentenced to life in prison with no possibility of parole, and Stefan took over as the new head of the agency and the family. It was still completely mind-blowing to me.

I didn't know if I would ever really get over it.

As I headed across the lobby toward the sleek bank of elevators, I waved to Jorge, our head of security.

"Morning, Emzee!" he said, waving back. "You look ready to kick some *culo* today."

He said that every day, about me kicking ass, and it always made me smile.

"You know I rock these shitkickers just to impress you," I said, shaking a combat boot for emphasis.

"You tease," he said. "I'm sure you have plenty of other men to impress."

Ha. If only. No men. No boys, even. The only males in my life are my brothers, Stefan and Luka. Well...and Ford, I guess. But he's definitely not impressed by me.

Technically, I *had* dressed up today, but not for Jorge. The truth was, the agency wasn't the only thing undergoing a change. From budding professional photographer to part-owner of my family's company, I knew I needed to start looking—and dressing—the part.

I still mostly wore black, but instead of jeans and artfully distressed T-shirts with a blazer or leather motor-cycle jacket on top, I had added a few actual suits and skirts to my closet. I'd never give up my big black boots, though. They were *me*.

And yeah, I didn't need to do much more than sit at a conference table today, but if the zombie apocalypse were to hit in the middle of a PowerPoint, you better believe I'd be ready for it. The only time I'd be caught in a pair of heels would have to be for a wedding (not mine, lol) or maybe a fancy date (which, ha. I wish.). Plus, they helped balance out my lack of height.

My suit was a perfectly tailored black St. John's with a pencil skirt and a silk blouse underneath. My dark hair was pulled over my shoulder in a fishtail braid instead of hanging loose around my face, which made my gray eyes stand out, and I'd applied my signature winged eyeliner and a touch of nude gloss. Anything more dramatic, I saved for nights out.

Not that I'd had many of those lately.

It would have been easy to blame my perpetually on-the-prowl status on my hectic work schedule—and I was more focused than ever now that we all had something to prove—but the truth was, I'd never been the kind of girl that settled down long-term. I could casually date until I was blue in the face, but rarely did I reach the point of being in an actual "relationship." Things always seemed to fall apart before then.

Probably for the best. Lord knows the media had devolved into a frenzy over the relationships of my older brothers. At least one of us Zoric children was happy to keep a low profile and stay out of the limelight.

The only exception was for my charity, See Yourself, which I'd founded to help former KZM models. I'd do just about anything to keep operations running. Including going out and getting attention.

The new clothes helped with that, too.

Still, I hated being noticed.

Growing up, I'd been told many times that I'd be a great asset to my father's company if I decided to give modeling a try. I couldn't do runway—I was too short for that—but, people suggested, I'd be great for print work. I was lucky to have inherited my mother's hourglass figure, and my entire Serbian family had been blessed with good looks.

But what was beauty, anyway? I'd grown up around models, around photographers, and around all the people that flocked to them. Beauty was fleeting, and subjective.

It could be dangerous, too.

That was something I'd learned from my father, even though I hadn't realized it at the time. I had simply never wanted to be stared at the way the KZ models were. Assessed. Admired. Objectified.

Shaking away my thoughts, I stepped into the elevator and jabbed the button that would take me up to the twenty-ninth floor. I checked my Shinola watch. Five minutes early. Excellent.

Stefan hadn't said much in his email last night. Just that we needed to have a family meeting, stat. I twisted the strap of my bag nervously between my fingers. With everything that had happened to the business—to our family—in the past year or so, I'd gotten used to these meetings being full of bad news. It didn't feel like today's would be any different.

Though things weren't all bad.

Ever since KZM had become Danica Rose, the atmosphere had changed. I came to work and saw smiling faces. People seemed more relaxed, no longer shrinking back every time my father stormed down the hallways. The models who had decided to stay with us (although technically, they signed new contracts with DRM) were happier, too.

And as for me and my brothers? For the first time, it felt like we were a real family. One that didn't keep secrets.

I'd always looked up to my brothers, and I knew they loved me, but we'd been raised very differently. I was the baby. Coddled, sheltered, and, in so many words, a bit spoiled.

Stefan and Luka, on the other hand, were brought up in my father's image, brought up to be a certain type of man. The type that was the head of a typical Eastern European family. The type that was like my father.

It created distance between us because their lives were so different than mine. Separate. I knew now that they'd been forced to do things they hated, that my father's special attention—especially the type he bestowed on Stefan, his heir—came with painful consequences. It had nearly cost our family everything.

Thankfully, our father was out of the picture, and things were heading in the right direction. Both of my brothers had married amazing, genius, incredibly decent human beings, and Tori and Brooklyn had changed my brothers' lives. And mine.

I'd wanted sisters my entire life, and with a few "I do"s, I got to have two.

Soon, they were both going to be mothers. I was going to be an aunt. Auntie Em.

I was beyond thrilled.

The elevator doors dinged open and I headed down the hallway with an extra bounce in my step, waving at our receptionist and a few agents, all who smiled and waved back at me. Knowing everything we'd gone through to get to this point, I felt a surge of pride.

No matter what Stefan had to say today, I knew I could hold on to that feeling.

Despite being a few minutes early, both Stefan and Luka were already waiting in the conference room when I swung the door open. Both of them looked tense. As expected.

"Morning," I chirped, trying to lighten the mood. "Is that carafe full, or do I need to swing by the break room for some fresh coffee?"

"Damien just dropped it off, along with some pastries," Luka said. "Help yourself."

Gosh, it would've been nice to have an assistant of my own at my beck and call. Always ready with the piping hot coffee and donuts. When I popped open the pink box, I locked eyes romantically with the guava cheese pastry, which I then snatched up before Stefan could grab it. Then

I took a huge bite and got comfortable in my chair, waiting for the verbal bomb to go off.

Stefan let out a long sigh.

"Whatever it is, I can handle it. Just spit it out," I said. "Also it's making me nervous that you're both standing there looming over me. Can you two sit down?"

They dropped into chairs across from me, but the vibe stayed anxious.

A year ago, the sight of both of my brothers in a conference room, side by side, ready for business, would have been a real shocker. Stefan had always been devoted to the company, sometimes to his own detriment, but Luka? Luka wouldn't have been caught dead doing anything resembling work when he could have been out banging models and getting drunk.

It was amazing how much they both had changed.

Now, Stefan wasn't living at the office, working around my father as he tried to find a way to save the women who were being trafficked through our company. My oldest brother was still busy as all get out, but he was devoted to Tori and I knew he was over the moon about the newest little addition that would be joining the family soon.

And Luka, well. He had finally stopped looking for himself at the bottom of a liquor bottle. He'd become a completely different person since marrying Brooklyn. Thank God for that.

There were times I felt a slight twinge of jealousy, knowing they got to go home at the end of the day to a partner who loved them, while all I was going home to was Munchkin.

I loved my rescued French bulldog—seriously adored him—but it wasn't quite the same.

Studying Stefan and Luka more closely, I realized that

something else was off. Usually Tori and Brooklyn were present for these family meetings. Not today, apparently.

Stefan adjusted his tie, took a sip of coffee, and then cleared his throat.

"We have a problem," he said. "A very big one."

Even though I'd been expecting it, my heart still sank.

"Of course we do. What is it this time?" Luka asked, running a hand over his face. He suddenly looked as nerve-racked as I felt. We'd been through so much over the past year, and every time things started getting better, we were hit with some heinous new catastrophe.

"This...is much worse than anything we've dealt with before," Stefan said. "I don't even know how to say it."

"If you could figure it out soon, it'd be much appreciated," I said dryly. "I have a nail appointment at noon."

Luka shot me an eye roll, which I knew I deserved, but you couldn't blame me for trying to insert a little levity after hearing something so heavy and ominous.

"This is the thing. Despite dismantling KZM's operations here in the US, the trafficking organization Dad was a part of is still active internationally," Stefan said. "It's thriving."

"Okay..." Luka said. "And this affects us how?"

Stefan's lips thinned into a hard line, and all of a sudden I thought I knew what was coming next. Dread curled low in my belly, and I pushed my pastry away, suddenly nauseated.

"The organization is not pleased that they've now lost one of their biggest outposts," Stefan went on. "I've been contacted by the Bratva."

Luka let out a long breath, and my jaw fell open. Even I knew who the Bratva were.

"The Russian mob?" I blurted. "Fuck. We're dead."

8

Stefan nodded. "We've cost them money with Danica Rose going legitimate, and they have now determined a dollar amount equivalent to what we owe them. Our debt, as they put it."

"This is bullshit!" Luka exploded. "We don't owe them a goddamn thing. We're not like KZ. We don't have to roll around in the muck with them anymore."

"Unfortunately, that is not how they see it," Stefan said.

He took out a piece of paper and wrote something on it.

"This is what they believe is owed to them," he said before passing it to Luka.

"*Jesus Christ.*" Luka looked like he was going to be sick. "This can't be real."

He passed it to me and my eyes bugged out at the number.

It was impossible.

We'd worked so hard, as a family, to get this business into the clear, to drag it free from my father's corrupt hands, and now this?

"We don't have this kind of money," I said. "And even if we did...we can't just hand it over to them."

"There must be something we can do," Luka said.

Stefan took the piece of paper from me and tore it into pieces.

"This information *does not* leave the room we're in," he said. "There's a reason that Tori and Brooklyn aren't here. They don't need to know anything about this. Got it?"

Luka and I nodded, even though I was barely paying attention. All I could think about was the money. That the Russian mob wanted. From us. The Bratva—the Brother-hood—was nothing to be fucked with. I knew the cruelty, the violence, the inhumanity they were capable of.

And I knew they wouldn't hesitate to act if someone got

in their way. Danica Rose Management was, apparently, in their way.

This was bad. Very, very bad.

Stefan said, "Look. I know this is..."

"Fucked," I finished for him. "Totally, completely, irrevocably *fucked*."

"Accurate. But the point is, we'll figure it out," he said, his expression softening a little.

I hated that so much of this fell on his shoulders. It didn't seem fair.

With that sense of dread and uncertainty hovering around us, we all left the conference room. My brothers went back to their executive suites. I went for a long walk.

Outside in the fresh Chicago air, all I wanted to do was call my best friend, my oldest friend. All I wanted was to talk to Ford, to tell him what was going on. He was more than just my friend...he was my hero. In all the years I'd known him, he'd always been the one other person (besides my brothers) that I could depend on. He'd always been there for me, and would go out of his way to come to the rescue and fix whatever problem I had. I trusted him completely.

But I couldn't trust him with this.

Not just because Stefan had made us promise to keep it secret. But because I knew that this was one thing that Ford couldn't fix. Maybe nobody could.

EMZEE

CHAPTER 1

Thankfully, what Ford couldn't fix, champagne could. At least temporarily.

I snagged a glass of bubbly off a passing tray, wishing that I could have stayed home and taken a nice bubble bath instead of getting dressed up to celebrate a woman who didn't even tolerate me, let alone like me.

But I hadn't come here for the birthday girl.

I had come for her son. For Ford.

As usual, the Malone family had gone all out for their matriarch's birthday. Ford's mother never saw an extravagance that she didn't immediately want for herself, and this party was no exception. It was black tie, of course, and the waiters were all gorgeous young men, wearing bespoke tuxedoes and carrying around equally expensive glasses of booze.

Even though fancy shindigs like this weren't really my style, I'd accepted the invitation hoping it would at least be fun. Beyond the endless flow of snazzy alcohol, these parties were legendary for how completely ridiculous they could get. The Malones knew everyone in Chicago—everyone *worth knowing*, as they say—so when they wanted to celebrate, things had a tendency to get crazy. Plus, there were always good anecdotes in the making, like how last year's soiree had ended in a million-dollar wager over a Connect Four game between the intoxicated CEOs of the city's two biggest hospitals.

The paparazzi would be waiting outside in droves afterward, hoping to get a shot of some drunk socialite or a couple investment banker bros throwing fists on the sidewalk.

I could already tell tonight was going to be epic, and that was even if no one did anything outrageous. The dinner would be a sit-down affair, as nothing so vulgar as a "buffet" would be appropriate for one of the wealthiest families in Chicago, and no doubt we'd be served the priciest gourmet cuisine money could buy. Followed by, I prayed, equally prime desserts.

Along with the glasses of Dom, there were silver platters circulating, each one covered with tiny, perfect hors d'oeuvres. I passed on the escargots de Bourgogne (snails aren't my fave, to be honest), but took full advantage of the latkes with caviar, brie en croute, and prosciutto-wrapped shrimp tartlets.

Like a glutton, I ate it all, down to the last crumb. I knew Ford's mother probably wouldn't touch a single morsel all night, and took perverse pleasure in knowing that she would probably hate the fact that I was enjoying her birthday food so much.

She didn't want me there, judging by the way she was glaring from across the room. She'd never liked that Ford and I were friends. My family's money was new, hers was old, and that was enough to make me trash in her eyes. On top of that, she was likely upset that Ford had brought me as his date tonight instead of his very, very longtime girlfriend, Claudia.

Or rather, his now *ex*-girlfriend.

I couldn't say I was sad about the breakup. Even though Claudia and Ford had been together for years and their families had been pushing them to get married almost from day one, I'd never gotten along with Claudia. It was a feeling that was entirely mutual.

She didn't like me because I was friends with Ford, and we had the kind of close friendship that someone like Claudia said was inappropriate between a man and woman. Not that she was jealous of me, or suspected any kind of infidelity. No, she made it perfectly clear that she didn't consider me any kind of threat whatsoever...she just didn't like that Ford spent so much time with me. That he and I shared more common interests than she and Ford did.

In my personal opinion, Claudia was a snobby, judgey bitch with no sense of humor.

Always had been.

I smoothed down my Givenchy gown. It was one of my favorite dresses, a sleek, form-fitting number with one long sleeve. The other sleeve was a simple strap that went across the bodice, then crisscrossed down the fabric in an edgy-artsy subtle design. And of course, my combat boots. Though the floor-length hem mostly covered them.

I also wore a gold bangle pushed up over my bare forearm and a pair of diamond briolette drop earrings that I'd had for years. Even still, I was probably the most modestly dressed woman in the room. The birthday girl, of course, was dripping in jewels, making sure to show every single one of her guests the chunky new diamond bracelet her husband had gifted her.

No doubt if Claudia had been in attendance, she would

have been hanging all over Ford, dropping hints that she'd like a bracelet like that. Maybe even a ring to match. Wink, wink.

Ford and I hadn't talked about it, but I wouldn't have been surprised if that was one of the main reasons they broke up. I knew Claudia was intent on settling down, and had been especially pushy about them getting engaged ever since her best friend had gotten married last spring, but he'd been dragging his feet for a while.

When he told me they'd split, I'd practically jumped for joy. Then I'd felt guilty. Because the real reason I'd been happy that he'd kicked Claudia to the curb had nothing to do with the fact that Claudia didn't like me or that Claudia was a sanctimonious mean girl.

It was the fact that I was, and always had been, totally and completely in love with Ford.

He had no idea, of course.

We'd been friends since sophomore year in high school, and I'd developed my crush on him then, but I'd kept my feelings a secret. Continued to keep them a secret. Because I knew that Ford didn't feel that way about me. He'd always dated girls like Claudia—old-money, tennis-playing, extroverted pretty girls who were just as comfortable riding their ponies at the country club as they were wearing ballgowns in the spotlight, who craved attention and popularity. I knew what he wanted, what he looked for in a woman, and it was not me.

We were just friends. We would always be just friends.

And honestly? That was enough for me. I wasn't the arm candy type, anyway.

After finishing my second flute of champagne, I retrieved another glass from a passing tray. There was a classical quartet in the corner, and though it wasn't really dancing music per se, I began swaying in time with the celloist.

I might have been a little tipsy. But I deserved it, didn't I? After the day I'd had.

Drinking more bubbly, I wondered where Ford had wandered off to.

I'd really hoped the evening would be a distraction from the news I'd gotten from Stefan this afternoon, but the number written on the piece of paper that he'd torn up still haunted me. There was no way we'd be able to pay off the Bratva. Surely they knew this, and I couldn't help worrying that they were already planning lots of horrible punishments, so they could make an example out of us to others in their network.

I shuddered at the thought.

It wasn't that I thought Ford would have a solution, it was just that it was killing me to keep it from him. We were friends, we helped each other out. Just like I was helping him this evening by essentially being a shield against his family's relentless questions about Claudia.

His mom didn't believe that it was over between them. According to Ford, she kept insisting that he was just looking to sow his wild oats before he finally settled down with Claudia. Despite the fact that he kept insisting just as stubbornly that they were done.

The thing was, I knew Ford's mother. She never took no for an answer. And if she wanted Claudia and Ford back together, then she'd do everything in her considerable power to make it happen. Hence, my presence tonight. I was here to distract Mrs. Malone as best I could and keep the peace.

I wasn't exactly sure how I was supposed to accomplish that, unless Ford actually meant for me to annoy his mother (something I could do in my sleep), rather than distract her.

At the very least, I'd been eager to spend time with Ford, but my date kept disappearing into the crowd. I knew he was hiding from his family, but the party was decidedly dull without him by my side.

Setting off into the largely older crowd, I tried to mingle. Events like these were usually perfect for shoring up support for my own charity; it was best to get rich people to agree to things while they were drunk and then shame them into their continued generosity later. But this time, I couldn't even muster the energy to shake down anyone for money.

Suddenly, I spotted an IG influencer who would be a fantastic fit for spreading the word about my charity. She was laughing and drinking and taking pictures of everything—especially herself. I knew I should cross the room and introduce myself. Still, my boots stayed put. I could barely muster the energy for a charming smile, let alone manage a coercive conversation.

Thankfully, that was when Ford chose to reappear.

I always needed a moment to collect myself when I saw him. Regardless of how long we'd known each other, he was just so unbelievably handsome with his mischievous smile, unruly chestnut brown hair, and liquid brown eyes. Plus those adorable deep dimples I was perpetually teasing him about, and that perfect angular jaw. Standing there in his tuxedo, he looked good enough to eat.

In all possible ways.

I sipped my champagne, feeling a flush come over me as my eyes raked over him from head to toe and then back up again. A girl could look, couldn't she?

"Having fun?" Ford asked, taking a drink from a glass of something that looked way darker and stronger than champagne.

I nodded, even though it was a lie. I was exhausted, and as much as I appreciated the sight of a cleanly shaven Ford in a tux with his hair smoothed back, smelling of cedar-esque cologne, I would honestly rather be spending the evening watching Netflix at home with my best friend, in a well-worn shirt and soft, broken-in jeans. The ones that molded to his ass perfectly.

It was hard to say what part of his body I liked the most. Those broad shoulders were the best for leaning on, and his big, strong arms made for some amazing hugs when they were wrapped around you. I guess he was just all around flawless. He was the kind of guy who took pride in the way he looked. He didn't spend all day at the gym, but he was athletic and strong.

Then again, I really loved those dimples. Maybe they were the best part of him. I always fought the desire to kiss them.

Aaand I was definitely a little drunk. These were the kinds of thoughts I allowed myself to entertain when I was alone in my bed at night with my trusty vibrator. My only lover, ever.

It was probably a little pathetic, being a virgin at twenty-three, but ever since I secretly gave my heart to Ford back in high school, I hadn't been able to find anyone that even came close to living up to him and the depth of our relationship. Sure, I'd had a few orgasms with guys, and I loved a good blowjob, but I just wasn't a casual sex kind of person. I was still stubbornly saving myself for someone I loved. Someone special. I didn't care that I was being either childishly romantic or stupidly old-fashioned about it. It was my choice.

"Thanks again for coming," Ford said, but he wasn't looking at me as he spoke.

His eyes were scanning the crowd. I knew he was looking for his mom, doing his damnedest to avoid her attempts to get him and Claudia back together, but I still felt invisible.

He hadn't even noticed that I'd been moody all evening —quiet and subdued and lacking my usual snarky sense of humor. It was something he'd normally remark on, but Ford was instead completely focused on himself and on hiding from his family.

Despite that, he seemed to be having a great time.

"Did you see the Bohlins?" he asked with a smirk. "They're having a massive fight over by the ice sculpture."

"Which one?" I asked, not really caring.

"The swan." Ford put his hand on my shoulder—the bare one—and turned me in the direction of the quarreling couple.

I did my best not to shiver at his touch.

"One hundred bucks, Mr. B gets stabbed with the swan's beak before the end of the evening. I think it's something to do with the au pair."

"Their British nanny?" Even though I was annoyed with him, I couldn't help smiling.

"That's the one. I'm going to get another drink," Ford said.

His glass was somehow empty already, but so was mine.

"I'll get us both a refill," he said, plucking my glass from my fingers.

I didn't need another drink and I really didn't want Ford to abandon me again, but he was gone before I could stop him. Watching him get joyfully waylaid by some friends, I realized he might be gone for a long time. Well. I couldn't really be mad at him. We weren't here together on an actual date or anything, so there was no need for him to stay glued to my side.

But that didn't mean I had to keep torturing myself like this.

No more, I told myself. *You can't keep being his second-string, doing him favors like this left and right. This is the last time.*

After tonight, I would have a talk with him. I'd make it clear that we needed to have better boundaries in our friendship, so it involved less of me being constantly at his beck and call and more of a 50-50 thing. I wouldn't keep running to him at the drop of a hat.

Suddenly, though, Ford was next to me again. He didn't have anything in his hand, so something must have happened on his way to the bar. It didn't take long to realize what that was.

His mother, trailed by two of his gossipy aunts and some family friends, was bee-lining straight for us.

"*Shit,*" he said under his breath, before turning on the charming smile I knew so well. "Mother," he said smoothly as she approached. "Happy Birthday. You look gorgeous."

"Happy Birthday, Mrs. Malone," I chimed in.

She ignored me, leaning forward to allow Ford to bestow a kiss on either cheek.

"Goodness, Ford darling, where's Claudia?" she asked, blinking innocently after making sure to give me a disapproving once-over.

Ford sighed. "Mom," he said. "I've told you a hundred times, we broke up."

"Did you?" she asked. "I must have forgotten."

I held back an eye roll at the blatant lie.

Meanwhile, Mrs. Malone turned to her other family members. "Oh, to be young again," she said. "Don't you remember all the romantic theatrics we put our parents through?"

"It's not theatrics," Ford said.

"Well, of course you'd *tell* yourselves that, but it doesn't mean it's truly over." His mother pouted, quite the feat for someone who'd had as much plastic surgery as her.

"Please, stop," Ford said. "Claudia and I are finished. I'm over her and I've moved on with my life. I suggest you do the same."

I felt Ford moving closer to me. This was where the protecting came in—if Mrs. Malone didn't let up, it would be my job to make up an excuse and politely drag Ford away with me.

"Moved on?" Ford's mother repeated, her eyes narrowing.

"That's what I said," he told her.

And then suddenly, his arm wrapped tight around my waist, and I was being pulled hard against his lean, muscular body.

"I'm with Emzee now."

EMZEE

CHAPTER 2

At first, I wasn't sure I'd heard him correctly.

Me? And Ford? *Together?*

No, I must have misheard. I'd allowed my fantasies to overload my reality. I was imagining things in my drunken state. Foolishly hoping for something I'd never actually have, but wanted desperately.

Then I clocked the expression on Mrs. Malone's face, which was truly a thing of beauty. To say that she looked shocked was a vast understatement. And I felt as stunned as she looked.

"Come on, dearest," Ford said, his arm still tight around my waist.

"You can't be serious," Mrs. Ford said, her voice dropping to a hiss.

She reached out and grabbed my arm, her diamond encrusted talons digging into my skin.

"Ouch," I said.

"Mother," Ford warned her, his tone steely. "Let go of Emzee."

She immediately released me, shooting eye-daggers in my direction.

"This won't stand," she sputtered as Ford's relatives began to close in, seeming to intuit that something untoward was going on.

The thought of them surrounding us, all their eyes on me, made me want to curl up in a ball or throw up or both. Thankfully, Ford pulled us out of the shrinking circle of people and out of the ballroom.

It wasn't until we were outside, with Ford's strong arms steering me around the pool and toward the bar, that I realized I still had the same fake, frozen smile stuck to my face.

"Ummm, Ford?" I somehow managed, speaking out of the corner of my mouth. "What the hell just happened?"

He laughed, as if this was all one big joke to him.

Yup, that was Ford in a nutshell—nothing fazed him. Everything was a good ol' time just waiting to happen.

"Just roll with it for now," he said, still holding me close. "It'd be a real solid. Besides, did you see her face?"

I couldn't help giggling aloud at the memory. "I wonder if it will stick like that."

Ford threw back his head and let out that infectious laugh of his.

"Serves her right," he said. "I hate the way she's always trying to meddle."

He pulled us over to the bar and ordered a Pappy Van Winkle, his favorite bourbon.

"Thanks again, Em," he said, releasing me to take a drink. "I really owe you one."

I deflated a little at that. I was supposed to be done doing solids for Ford, dammit. For anyone, really, but especially him.

Yet I couldn't deny that it felt good to be laughing together and sharing a secret. It was always these moments that kept me coming back, even when he'd ditch me for Claudia or get careless about returning my calls. Or forget my birthday. Ford would always make it up to me later, layering on an extra helping of charm to smooth things over.

This, though—our banter and our shared history—was real.

So for now, I'd be the good friend. I'd roll with the punches. If doing him a favor meant pretending to be his girlfriend, well, maybe it wasn't too much of a hardship after all.

"Come on," Ford said, finishing his bourbon with one long swallow.

I tried not to stare at him while he did, but it was hard not to admire how good he looked tonight. His hair was looking a little more tousled than before...he'd probably been running his hands through it. The thought made me want to run *my* hands through it, but before I could accidentally reach out, Ford grabbed my hand and pulled me back into the throng.

People were eager to talk to him and we wove through the crowd, carefully avoiding his mother and other family members who seemed to always be appearing and disappearing out of the corner of my eye.

"Who shall I introduce you to next, dearest?" Ford asked. "I'm going to make sure you get the complete girlfriend experience."

Did it make me pathetic that I got butterflies every time he called me dearest? Even knowing full well it was for show?

"Oh, no, it's okay," I said. "I'm fine."

"Lies," he said with a grin, shaking his head. "I know you came here at least partly to raise some funds for your charity."

I was a little touched that he remembered.

"I came here for *you*," I said. "Because you asked."

"I know," he said. "But I also know you're relentless when it comes to your causes. So who can we squeeze some money out of?"

He looked positively gleeful at the thought and I couldn't help but laugh. Whenever Ford was like this—a little drunk and a lot eager—fun and crazy things usually happened. In fact, I wouldn't have been surprised to discover that he was the one behind the epic Connect Four game last year. He always managed to stir up trouble wherever he went.

"You pick the target," I said. "I'll just play along."

"Aww, come on," he coaxed. "I know you. I'd bet anything you have your eye on someone already."

I laughed, feeling my cheeks go warm. He did know me.

"Okay," I confessed. "I *might* have been checking out Jessie Flores."

Ford scrunched up his nose. "Who?"

I gave him a look. "You'd recognize her. She's a huge influencer."

The look of confusion didn't fade from his handsome face.

"She's all over social media," I tried again. "Takes pictures of herself doing, like, yoga poses in a bikini at national parks or in front of beautiful monuments."

Recognition sparked in Ford's eyes. "BikiniBliss? I love her pictures."

I rolled my eyes.

"Yeah, I'm sure it's her pictures that you're admiring when you double tap," I said.

He held up his hands. "What do you expect?" he said. "I have eyes."

"You think you can keep it in your pants long enough to spark up some friendly conversation, or am I better off flying solo?" I asked.

"We got this. Where is she?" Ford asked, craning his neck as he looked across the ballroom for her.

"Gah, stop being so obvious!" I grabbed his arm. "She's over there, by the ice sculpture."

"The swan again? That thing's been a magnet for all the who's-who tonight."

"No, the other one. I think it's an eagle or something," I said.

"I don't get my mother's obsession with birds," he said, still looking. "It's downright creepy."

I giggled.

"There she is," Ford said.

"Your mother?"

"No, your influencer. And it's not an eagle, it's my mother's spirit animal. A vulture."

I couldn't help but laugh as Ford dragged me across the room toward Jessie.

"Ford, wait," I hissed. "I don't know her. I can't just walk up to her and ask for money."

"If you can't, I will," Ford said. "And besides, it looks like she's got a sugar daddy boyfriend, so if she isn't into it, maybe I can squeeze a few bucks out of him."

That's when I noticed that Jessie was standing with an older man—who could have easily passed as her father if not for the possessive hand he had resting on her ass.

"Well that's something you don't see on her Instagram," I said dryly.

Ford shrugged. "Whatever floats your boat. Maybe he's a yogi, too. He definitely looks like he's got the whole zen thing down."

I couldn't help smiling. Very few things bothered Ford. A May-December romance between a semi-famous influencer and some old rich dude was barely a blip in his world.

"Off we go," he said and took my hand.

That was nice. The hand-holding. Even if it was all for show.

Confident as ever, Ford strolled right up and introduced himself.

"You're Jessie Flores, right?" he asked. "I love your IG account. You've really found a way to elevate yoga, open more eyes to the art and soul of it all."

Trying not to gag, I nodded along with his smarmy compliments.

Jessie blushed, tossing her braids over her shoulder. "I hope so," she said.

"Beautiful stuff," Ford added. "This is my girlfriend, Emzee, by the way."

She nodded at me, her smile dimming just a little, but mine bloomed. I hated that I got such a thrill out of this dumb, pretend game that Ford and I were playing.

"Emzee's also a huge fan of your work," Ford said.

"That is so flattering," Jessie said.

"I'm a professional photographer as well," I told her. "You have such a wonderful eye for color and form."

Her smile ramped back up again. "Thank you," she said. "This is my boyfriend, Jonathan."

The older man reached out and shook Ford's hand.

"Jonathan Albright?" Ford asked. "Of the Albright Foundation?"

My eyes nearly bugged out of my skull. The Albright Foundation was involved with nearly every worthwhile charity in Chicago. I'd been dying to get them interested in mine.

"Indeed," Jonathan said, looking around the room appreciatively. "Your mother certainly knows how to throw a party."

"That she does," Ford said. "But enough about my mother."

Everyone laughed, and Ford put his arm around me.

"Emzee runs an amazing charity that works with women transitioning into new careers in photography; perhaps you've heard of it. It's called See Yourself."

Jessie looked interested. "Wait, I've heard of them. That's your organization?"

I nodded, grateful for Ford for teeing me up as well as he had.

"We're always looking for talented photographers like yourself to volunteer," I said. "We offer classes, one- and two-day workshops, and longer-term mentorship programs, and if you're interested, I think you'd really be able to make a difference with our mentees."

I knew I was laying it on a bit thick, but I also knew that people like Jessie reacted well to excessive praise. The growing smile on her face confirmed that I'd utilized the right tactic.

"Omigosh, that sounds wonderful," she said. "I'd love to teach a workshop!"

"Brilliant. Let me give you my card," I said, pulling one out of my Chanel bag.

Ford gave me a little nudge as I handed it over.

"And you're currently looking for additional benefactors, isn't that right?" he said.

I nodded.

"We are." I turned my attention to Jonathan. "Your organization is so highly regarded, I think we could join forces and help even more people."

"Oh Jonathan, you have to!" Jessie cooed.

Minutes later, I had Jessie's workshop availability in my calendar and the promise of a fat donation check from Jonathan. Walking away, I felt like I was on the top of the world.

"Thank you," I said to Ford, still hardly believing it. "Thank you so much."

He shrugged. "I just made the introductions. You did the rest."

"I couldn't have done it without you," I said, beaming.

"You're very welcome, then. Now come on," he said, looping his arm around my waist. "Let's see if we can't get you a few more donors."

It was different, doing this as a team, being on Ford's arm.

The crowd parted as we walked through it, people whispering about us, vying for our attention. So many pairs of eyes were on me, but I didn't mind it as much as I would have thought. Because people actually seemed to *see me* when they thought I was his. I loved it.

And I hated that I loved it.

All of this was a sweet sort of pain. I knew it was just an act—that, to him, it was just a way to keep his mother from harassing him about Claudia. A way to annoy her and his family.

Even so, I couldn't help being affected by his touch. The way he would stroke my arm as we chatted with the guests, the way he kept resting his hand on my hip. At one point in the evening, he'd even dropped an affectionate kiss on the top of my head.

It was heaven, yes, but knowing that it was all fun and games for Ford meant that there would be emotional hell for me to pay later.

I tried to convince myself it was worth it.

EMZEE

CHAPTER 3

The thing about cake is, it makes pretty much everything better.

Even shamefully extravagant parties for snobby, aging socialites who hated the idea of me dating their son.

I managed to keep a smile pasted on my face for the rest of the party, including while singing "Happy Birthday" to Mrs. Malone. Her cake—a surprisingly delicious, towering confection comprised of flourless Calamondin orange layers topped with cream cheese glaze and sugared edible flowers —went a long way toward improving my mood, which lasted all the way through the goodbyes at the end of the evening.

Finally, though, Ford escorted me out of the ballroom. Down we went to the car he'd ordered to take us home to our separate apartments, me snuggling my head against his shoulder with his jacket draped over me, trying to squeeze every last drop I could out of the fantasy. But the second the driver shut the car door behind us, I let my smile drop.

I couldn't pretend anymore.

It was time to have The Discussion. Just because I rolled with the whole faux-dating routine for the duration of the party didn't mean that I planned to continue letting him walk all over me. I had to stay strong, stick to my earlier vow to change the basic tenets of our friendship.

To be fair, I knew it was as much my fault as his. We had a certain power dynamic between us, had been playing this game since our high school days. Ever since he saved me from the prep school bullies who called me a whore and a slut, who would literally corner me while I was changing for gym so they could talk shit and mock my early-bloomer body.

Even now, years later, I had no idea how the rumors got started. Sure, I was the only ninth grader wearing a C-cup, but ever since I'd hit puberty around the age of twelve, I'd done everything I could to downplay my chest. Still, it was the only reason I could think of that someone had decided to target *me*—basically an antisocial virgin who barely left the house—and tell the entire school that I was meeting up with random men from the internet, blowing guys under the bleachers for cash, and screwing the entire football team at their post-game keg parties.

It didn't matter to anyone at my school that there was zero evidence, that all of it was a complete lie. Everyone believed the rumors. Everyone thought I was trash. People would throw crumpled one-dollar bills and heckle me whenever they could get away with it. It was horrible.

The worst was when someone—or maybe multiple someones—filled my locker with condoms. I opened it in the middle of the day, when the hallways were full of people, so practically the whole school saw a mountain of condoms avalanche onto the floor onto my shoes. I'd slammed my locker and fled, but the sound of laughter had followed me, echoing in my ears.

In sum, my freshman year had been a nightmare. Until two things happened.

First, my older brother Stefan had taken me to his senior prom as his "date." Before that, I'd been nothing but an outcast freshman who the mean girls loved to torture. After prom, though, people actually knew who I was. Namely, the younger sister of Stefan (and Luka) Zoric. But even though Luka and I grew close after Stefan left for college that summer, Luka definitely didn't protect me at school. He barely showed up for classes to begin with, and when he did? He was more interested in chasing girls than looking out for his vaguely goth loner of a little sister.

So, secondly, and I suppose even more importantly (since Stefan was gone, leaving me to battle my way through another agonizing three years of high school without him making me seem cool by proxy), Ford Malone started hanging out with me. Sticking up for me. Shutting down the trolls and bullies one by one like he was my own personal bodyguard. Hence the hero thing. Hence my undying devotion. Hence this hideous, unkillable crush.

I returned the favor by writing an English term paper for him our sophomore year, and ever since then, we'd become the person who did the other's dirty work. Even so, the scars from the bullying never really faded. It was part of the reason I didn't like to be the center of attention.

"That party wasn't half bad," Ford mused, looking out the window as the streets of Chicago—so beautiful, the way they were lit up at night—sped by.

"Yeah," I said, still lost in my head and trying to figure out where to start.

"You made a lot of contacts. Lots of money heading your way for See Yourself."

I nodded and felt a little twinge of guilt about what I was about to say. Because he was right; I *had* gotten a lot accomplished in terms of networking and fundraising. It was going to make a huge difference to the organization as we moved forward. And I was grateful for that.

But.

"We need to talk, Ford," I said, trying to keep my tone as neutral as possible.

He had leaned his head back against the seat, eyes now closed.

"Mmm," he murmured.

It was clear he was about to fall asleep. I couldn't really blame him. I was exhausted too. A little drunk, socially overexerted, and my feet hurt. Truth be told, I would rather finish this ride in silence, get home, and slide into a hot bath with a glass of water and two Advil.

However, this conversation had waited long enough.

"Ford," I said more firmly, giving him a nudge.

He opened his eyes and looked at me. "What?"

"What did you do that for tonight?" I asked.

"Do what for?"

"The lie," I clarified. "About us dating."

That lazy grin stretched across his face as he said, "It was the obvious solution, no?"

I let out a sigh. "The *obvious solution* would have been to change the subject with your mom. Not to lie to her about us being a couple."

Ford shifted in his seat, turning to face me. He'd loosened his tie at some point, leaving his shirt unbuttoned at the throat. That flash of bare skin drew my eyes like a magnet.

"Are you pissed at me?" he asked point-blank.

"It's not that," I told him. "But now you're going to have to admit to her that you lied, which is going to be awkward for everyone. Not to mention how pissy she'll be with me for going along with this little scheme of yours—and on her birthday no less." I crossed my arms over my chest. "Your mom already hates me, so this isn't going to help things."

"First of all, my mom doesn't like anyone," Ford said.

"She likes Claudia," I reminded him. "She *loves* Claudia."

Ford winced, but then visibly brightened.

"That's exactly why this is so genius," he said. "Don't you see?"

"I see that your mom is going to be furious," I said.

"No, no, no. Wait a second," Ford said, excitement lighting his eyes. He always got like this when he was coming up with schemes. "Dude, it's the perfect plan."

I would bet my life on it that he'd never called Claudia, "dude." She probably would have slapped him if he tried.

"What is?" I asked, knowing full well that I was already halfway to saying yes.

"You can just *pretend* to *actually* be my girlfriend for a little while. Think about it! It'll be completely believable, and rebounds never last anyway—it'll just be a few weeks so I can get a break from all my mom's nagging."

"Your rebound," I echoed hollowly.

Ford slid closer to me, clasping his hands in mock prayer. "Please, Emzee. I'm begging you. I need a breather! You don't know how bad it's been."

"I mean, I have an idea..." I told him.

He shook his head. "Before the breakup she was trying to give me my great-grandmother's engagement ring to propose to Claudia with. She'd even picked out baby names for her future grandchildren! Farrah Edith and Bentley Sedgwick."

"Sounds awful," I said dryly.

"It really is." Ford scrubbed his face, a desperate air coming over him. "Look, I just need to convince her that the Claudia ship has definitely sailed."

"I think it's a bad idea." And I wasn't much for lies. Just look how they'd destroyed my family, the fabric of untruths my father had woven around us. My brothers and I were still repairing the damage he had done. I knew exactly how toxic lying could be.

Ford went on as if I hadn't even spoken. "You and I can go back to dating other people in a few weeks. A month or two, tops. Say yes."

Dammit. The second he'd said, "dating other people," it had set off a chain reaction in my head—and my stupid, naïve heart.

It wasn't like I thought the breakup with Claudia meant that he was suddenly seeing me in a new light...but at the same time, I really didn't like the idea of him swiping right on other girls, and maybe finding that new light in a stranger instead. Because it was obvious Ford was shooting for a rebound either way. It could be me, or it could be some rando.

I looked out the window of the car. The streets were quiet, the brownstones looking cozy with golden light glowing from inside, Chicago's iconic skyline silhouetted in the distance. The whole world seemed kind of magical. Like it was just me and Ford, flying through the city.

"I need you, Em," he whispered.

My heart skipped a beat. Dammit. Reluctantly, I said, "I'll think about it. Just give me a few days."

"Yes!" Ford crowed.

As if I had ever told him no before.

As if this time would be any different.

Deep down, I knew I'd already made my decision.

"A month?" I repeated.

Nodding, he said, "Two max. You'll be back on the market in no time, I promise."

"Well that's a relief," I said sarcastically.

The car pulled to a stop outside my building. As the driver got out to come around and open the door, Ford pulled me into a tight hug.

"You're the best," he said, his breath warm against my hair. "I'll call you."

A part of me wondered if he was still drunk—if this whole thing was just a whim or some impulse he'd forget all about by tomorrow morning. Only time would tell.

Stepping into my loft, I realized I still had Ford's jacket over my shoulders. So I did what I'd wanted to do in the car, pulling it closer and taking a deep breath. It smelled like him, of course, a woodsy vetiver scent, mixed with a faint hint of the bourbon he'd been drinking.

Hearing the click-clack of tiny toenails on hardwood, I looked up to find my dog Munchkin trotting toward me, a silly grin stretched across his face.

"Hi, you little mush!" I greeted him, setting his stubby tail a-wagging.

After sweeping his little bulldozer body up into my arms, I burrowed my face into his soft black fur. It was hard to believe he and his littermates had been rescued, half frozen to death, from a downtown dumpster in the middle of winter. Not for the first time, I thought about how lucky we were to have found each other.

"What do you think about me pretend-dating Ford for a month?" I asked.

Munchkin, of course, had no verbal response, but he did let out a huff.

"It's going to be fine," I whispered, even though I knew, deep down, it wouldn't be.

Because I knew that Ford Malone was going to break my heart.

EMZEE

CHAPTER 4

"Em? Earth to Emzee?" A gentle voice pulled me back to reality. "You okay?"

I glanced up to find my sister-in-law Tori standing by our table at NoMI, looking a little concerned. She was wearing a designer maternity dress, a floral wrap maxi with little bows on the sleeves, and as usual she looked radiant.

"Yeah, no, I'm fine," I fibbed, standing to greet her. "Also you look amazing, mama. Have some breadsticks before I finish them all, they're to die for."

Tori grabbed one and bit into it with a grin. "I feel like that bratty girl in Willy Wonka's factory who turned into a giant blueberry, but thanks for the compliment."

We exchanged cheek kisses before sitting down. It took her a little longer to get into the booth than it did me, lowering herself carefully, her belly huger than I'd ever seen it.

"So how's things?" she asked. "Have you, umm, had any contact with your dad?"

I shook my head. "I don't even know if that's going to

happen, honestly. I need some time. He'll always be my dad, but...it's still kind of a mindfuck. You spend your whole life around someone and you think you know them, and then...you realize you don't. At all."

She nodded. "I get it. Really. And I won't push. Just know I'm here if you want to talk. Stefan's been a mess, too."

It wasn't just dad-in-jail stuff that had me in a slump. After last night's whirlwind of emotions with Ford, I was really counting on my bi-monthly Lunch With The Wives (that's how I had it down in my calendar) to be the distraction I so desperately needed.

Having grown up in a house full of men, I appreciated the fact that the family now included Tori and—more recently—Brooklyn, my brother Luka's wife. No more boys' club for me. Still, it was an adjustment. For someone used to being around a bunch of emotionally distant males, it was taking me some time to warm up to the idea of being completely open with my sisters-in-law. Mostly I let them spout their troubles and humble brags and pregnancy anecdotes while I pretended they weren't talking about my older brothers. Because ew.

"Your charcuterie board and wine," the waiter said cordially, dropping off the items I'd ordered. "May I get you started with something?" he asked Tori.

"I'd love a mocktail," she said. "Something fruity?"

As they chatted about the faux-alcohol selection, my mind immediately reverted back to Ford and our conversation last night. Could I survive pretending to be his girlfriend for a month, possibly two? What if it made our friendship weird? What if I got too attached to the ruse, and couldn't act normal around him afterward? It seemed so risky...but maybe worth the risk?

That was when Brooklyn showed up, calling out our names across the restaurant as she wove through the tables. Even without the verbal announcement, it would have been hard not to notice her; as a top Danica Rose model and popular social media influencer, not only was she breathtakingly beautiful, but she knew how to make an entrance.

It was part of what made Brooklyn who she was. She was all about "moments"—appreciating them, capturing them, and sharing them. They were the focus of her IG account, and her followers loved the vicarious experiences they "lived" via her posts. Whenever she taught classes for my charity, I got great feedback. Taking photos for social media was very different from artistic or commercial photography, and she was really, really good at what she did.

"Sorry I'm late," she whispered as she slid into the booth next to me.

She wasn't as far along in her pregnancy as Tori, but thanks to her bodycon dress, I couldn't help noticing that Brooklyn's cute little baby bump was getting a lot rounder.

"One blueberry rosemary lemon mocktail," the waiter said, repeating Tori's order back to her. "And for you?" He turned to Brooklyn.

"That sounds so good—I'll have the same," she said with a grin. "Oh, and an order of the lobster beignets, please. Thank you!"

They immediately launched into a discussion about morning sickness, which Brooklyn was only just starting to experience in full force, and I nodded along and tried not to think about Ford Malone. Stupid Ford Malone. Stupid, gorgeous, dimpled, always-gets-what-he-wants—

"Emzee?"

My head whipped up and I realized I'd zoned out again.

Tori and Brooklyn were both staring at me expectantly, obviously awaiting a response to some question.

"Sorry, what?" I said.

Brooklyn smiled. "You've really got your head in the clouds today, don't you? This is the first time I've ever seen you not snap to attention the second something about food comes up."

Tori leaned over and pointed at the menu in front of me that I've been ignoring. "We were trying to figure out if we should blow our seafood limit for the week getting every kind of sushi they have or just gorge ourselves on burgers and French onion soup."

"That's a tough call, because there is no wrong choice here," I said seriously. "But I'm leaning burger myself. Maybe with avocado and a side of heirloom carrots."

"Mmmm," they moaned in unison.

Once our order was in, I tried my hardest to pay attention to the conversation despite my obsession over the Ford thing. His timing could not have been worse, honestly.

Something about both of my brothers being married (with babies on the way, no less) had made me think it was finally time to get over my crush on Ford. So I'd recently decided to get out there and try dating for real. Meaning I'd force myself to go out with other mature, well-adjusted adults who had similar views and life goals and interests— instead of letting myself fall for every hot, immature, self-absorbed artist within a ten-hour flight time radius who piqued my interest, and then a few months later asking myself (yet again) how it had managed to blow up in my face so badly. Because, yes, that was my usual pattern.

It was time to change it up.

And I'd really been ready. I'd really wanted to try. I'd signed up for a few dating apps to psych myself up, and I'd even been accepted to Reva. My thought was that the exclusive matchmaking service would mean my dates were pre-vetted, so it'd be easier to find someone who not only lived up to my brothers' insanely high standards, but who'd also be as passionate about and successful in his trade as I was. It had seemed like the perfect plan to move on from my best friend.

But how was I supposed to do that now if I was pretending to date him?

God, and how could I still be obsessing over this petty stuff when the Bratva's threats were still hanging over my family's heads? Not that Tori and Brooklyn knew anything about it. Everything was just a mess.

"You know I love you," Brooklyn said, "but I refuse to sit here while you stew in silence, Em. So whatever it is, you're either going to have to spit it out now or worry about it later."

My fake smile was instantaneous. "I'm fine. It's just... work stuff."

Tori narrowed her eyes. "What kind of work stuff? Is something happening with the agency? Stefan's seemed kind of avoidant lately. I thought I was just being paranoid, but..."

There's no way I could let her or Brooklyn get suspicious about the Bratva stuff, and the last thing they needed right now was to find out how much trouble we were in. Quickly, I changed the subject—by blurting out the truth. "Just having some dating drama."

"What?!" Tori blurted excitedly. "I didn't know you were seeing anyone!"

Brooklyn scooted closer. "Are you having boy troubles?" She tilted her head, frowning a little. "Or girl troubles? No judgement here."

"I'm not exactly seeing anyone per se, but..." At the thought of Ford's proposition, I could feel my cheeks heat, but I was in too deep now. I'd just have to spill my guts.

"But..." prodded Tori.

Searching their faces, I said, "Okay, you have to swear that this is all Vault, okay? Like, do not repeat this to anyone including your inner circle. It's kind of humiliating."

"Of course," Brooklyn agreed, nodding.

"We swear ourselves to utmost secrecy and discretion," Tori put in. "Cross our hearts."

"Okay." I took a deep breath and scooted closer. "So here's the thing. Last night, one of my best guy friends asked me if I'd agree to fake-date him for a month or two. To get his mom off his back about his ex, because she's been tormenting him. I don't really know the terms except that we can't see other people, but I'm torn. I'm still mulling it over."

There. I'd said it. Maybe it'd do me some good to have a few other opinions about it. Besides, they weren't wrong; I was obviously brimming with angst over the situation.

"Should I help him out?" I asked. "It seems risky."

"Risky how?" Brooklyn said. "You don't have feelings for him, do you?"

"No, of course not," I said, quickly stuffing my face with a bite of cheeseburger to avoid blurting anything incriminating.

Tori swiped a few of my fries, having already devoured hers. "Isn't that all the more reason to help him out, then? It's just temporary. Are you attracted to him?"

Setting my food back down, I shrugged. "I mean, anyone who sees him is attracted to him. But he's my best friend. We've known each other since high school, and I'm fond of him. Just not like that."

"Still, that's a fun bonus. Why turn down free arm candy? Maybe you could even use him to make other guys jealous when you go out," Tori mused.

"I think you should go for it, Em," Brooklyn said. "And since he's hot, you should definitely bang him and report back. You're young and single. Might as well make it fun."

She and Tori laughed, and I tried to join in.

"I definitely will *not* be banging him, but I appreciate the advice," I said. Then I changed the subject to the dessert menu, insisting they save room for the caramel pots de creme.

Obviously there was no way in hell I could sleep with Ford. That would be the real risk. Because I'd never confess it to The Wives, but the honest truth was...I still had my V-card. Giving it up to Ford would definitely not help with my Feelings.

But damn. Fantasizing about it couldn't hurt, could it?

EMZEE

CHAPTER 5

As soon as I woke up to Munchkin's little head butting against my side, urging me to get up and give him his walk and his breakfast, I knew I was out of time. Today was the day I'd said I'd give Ford an answer by. And after ignoring his calls yesterday, I knew I couldn't hide. I had to face him. Soon.

Drat.

Groaning, I rolled out of bed and let my furbaby lead the way to his leash, his chubby little butt wiggling with excitement. Sure, it wasn't even 7 a.m. yet on a Sunday, but there were two males in this world that I couldn't say no to —my French bulldog, and Ford Malone.

After making Munchkin sit and stay like a good boy, I clipped his leash to his studded collar and took him for a leisurely trot around the neighborhood. No matter how many times we took this route, he always seemed to get a kick out of sniffing the same exact spots. I spent most of the walk trying to psych myself up for the Talk with Ford.

Could I say no to him? Did I want to? What was the best course of action?

Would I have more regrets about not going through with this and missing my chance to "date" Ford, or about agreeing to the fake-dating plan and then having my heart crushed later?

In the end, there was no point in pretending I wasn't going to go along with his foolhardy plan. I knew I could either own my decision and do my best to enjoy our short time as a couple, or I could spend the entire course of our faux relationship worrying about my emotions.

You got this, I silently pep-talked myself. *Just have fun and keep your heart out of it.*

Easier said than done, obviously.

By the time Munchkin and I were back at the loft, his attention fully focused on his food dish, I was as ready as I'd ever be. But I planned to make it very clear that this would be the last time. After this favor, things would have to change. I couldn't keep thinking of him as my hero, and he couldn't keep treating me like his wingman. We needed to be equals going forward. Assuming, of course, that our friendship managed to survive this farce.

I hoped Ford realized that a fake relationship could have just as many real consequences as a legitimate one, especially if anyone found out what we were up to.

Feeling like I was readying for battle, I dried my hair, pulled it up into a sky-high Ariana Grande ponytail, and then put on my Most Serious Makeup: my winged eyeliner, smoky shadow, three coats of super volumizing waterproof mascara, and a delightfully intimidating shade of burgundy lip gloss. Then I put on my power suit: black pinstripe with a matching vest and blazer that had slightly puffed sleeves. Instead of a button-up shirt, I wore a lacy camisole underneath that just barely peeked out from the V-neck of the vest. It was a combination of sexy and fierce; the outfit I wore when I needed the kind of confidence that I usually only got when I was behind the lens on a photo shoot. Time to kick some *culo*.

Taking one last look at myself in the mirror, I dialed Ford.

"Hey!" he said, picking up on the first ring. "Glad you called. I couldn't reach you yesterday."

My heart leapt. "Yeah, about that. I was thinking we should talk some more."

"Yeah, definitely," Ford said breezily. "What's up?"

"I, umm..." This was no time to be losing my nerve.

But then I heard the sound of other voices in the background. Where was he?

"Why don't you meet me here at the club?" he said. "Tennis and lunch. You'll love it."

Then he hung up. Deflated, I looked at my reflection. So much for my makeup and outfit.

After swiping off my dark lip and toning down my eye makeup, I grudgingly changed into my tennis whites (thanks to my family, I did indeed own some). I might not enjoy going to the country club for sport, but I knew how to dress for it. Even if I hated wearing all this white.

I drove over, valeted my convertible, and then walked inside. It was easy enough to find Ford. He was sitting at the bar with a martini in his hand, and he wasn't alone. Instead, he was surrounded by a group of guys, loudly holding court —all of them were laughing and drinking and having a great time. There was no way we'd be able to talk about our fauxlationship.

Sighing, I almost turned and left, but then Ford's face lit up as he spotted me across the room. I couldn't help obeying when he waved me over.

"Guys," Ford announced, looping an arm around my

waist and pulling me against his strong, hard body. "This is the new girlfriend I was telling you about! Emzee, these are some of my colleagues from the real estate office."

Ah. So, just like always, Ford had taken me for granted and assumed I'd agree to his plan. I never said no to him, though, so why would I this time?

Still, he didn't have to make it so damn obvious that he was in the driver's seat—again. I was already feeling on edge, and even his little public display of snuggling (as good as it might have felt) wasn't going to completely erase my irritation. At both him *and* myself.

I didn't know who I was more annoyed with.

"So nice to meet you all," I simpered. "I've heard such great things."

As they returned to their conversation, I tried to act interested, already playing the part of doting girlfriend just like Ford had obviously assumed I would. I always bailed him out, covered for him, lied for him, everything—of course I did. I was in love with him. But it was starting to occur to me that loving Ford had a higher cost than I realized.

Namely, my own well-being.

But I kept up my smile, fully committed to playing along as the guys joked and laughed. Because that's what I do. Meanwhile, Ford's hands never lingered too far from my hip or my shoulder. He started playing with my ponytail at a certain point, giving it these taut little tugs that I kind of liked. Okay, that I *really* liked.

My body was at complete odds with my mind.

"You look great in that tennis skirt, babe," Ford said loudly, dropping a kiss on my temple. "Good enough to eat."

I flushed. "I was actually surprised I could still get into this outfit, I haven't played tennis in so long."

"She looks amazing, doesn't she?" Ford took my hand

and made me do a little twirl in front of the guys. "All bright-eyed and bushy-tailed on a Sunday morning."

They all nodded and voiced their agreement.

"Can't even tell that I had her up. All. Night. Long." Ford offered a leering wink and all the guys laughed.

I could feel my face getting even hotter.

"Oh you," I said, gritting my teeth, giving him a harder-than-necessary swat on the arm.

"Look at that," Ford said, rubbing his arm as he grinned back at me. "She can still blush. Gotta love a girl that's innocent in the streets and wild in the sheets, am I right?"

Everyone chuckled. Ford raised his glass—he obviously wasn't the only one who'd been doing a little day drinking—and his coworkers did the same, all of them clinking their glasses together with frat boy-esque solidarity.

Who the hell was he trying to impress? These guys were all technically his employees, since Ford was already VP at Malone Real Estate Holdings. Despite his age, which probably rankled them since they were all twice as old (and twice as experienced), they *had* to pretend they liked him. He was the boss. There was no need to parade me—or "us" —around like this.

Without warning, his hand snaked around my waist, sliding down until it rested on my ass. Then he gave it a firm squeeze. I jumped. Ford had never touched me like that before.

"Ford!" I hissed, less than discreetly.

"What?" he asked, all innocence.

Enough was enough. Time to either take control of the situation or get the hell out of there.

"Well, *honey*, it's obvious you've had more than enough drinks to loosen you up," I told Ford, pretending to appreciatively squeeze his bicep while purposely digging my nails into it. "So why don't we go play that tennis match you promised me? Or would you rather I go find someone else to play games with?"

Despite my teasing tone, my warning was clear. He could get up right now and play nice with me, or I was done with this charade. Which had lasted all of twenty minutes so far.

I dug into his arm a little harder for emphasis as he rose from his seat.

"All right, all right, easy there tiger," he said, reaching over me to give one of the guys a high five. "I like a woman who knows what she wants. Let's go."

Even with a few drinks in him, Ford was able to easily beat me at tennis. Which was fine with me, since I wasn't actually there to play.

"Okay. I've made my appearance, we've officially been seen on the court together, and now I'm going home," I told him from the other side of the net.

He frowned. "Wait, but what about lunch? You just got here."

"I'm really not hungry. But *you* should probably eat something before you embarrass yourself in front of your coworkers any worse," I said. "And do yourself a favor: take an Uber home."

With that, I stalked off the court.

Later that night I was still frustrated and annoyed, even after I'd edited a round of recent DRM photos and made lemon pasta and salmon for dinner. I tried to walk it off by taking Munchkin on a jog afterward, but if anything I was even more wound up by the time we got home. Exhausted, he plopped down on his bed in the living room and started snoring almost instantly while I cleaned up all the dinner dishes in the kitchen. After I showered, I burrowed under my covers, replaying Ford's actions at the country club in my mind.

I didn't understand what he was trying to prove. But while my rational brain still had misgivings about his methods, my body couldn't stop remembering how it felt to be touched by him. The way his hands had trailed hotly over the curves of my hips, my waist, my ass.

He'd behaved himself during our tennis match, further proving that his comments had all been for show, but now, alone in my apartment, I couldn't help pretending the sexual innuendos were real. That last night, the two of us really had done all the things he'd insinuated.

All. Night. Long.

I got hot just thinking about it, tension making my stomach tight, forcing me to squeeze my thighs together against the ache there. What would it be like for Ford to take my virginity? For him to push me against a wall and kiss me, his hands going up my skirt, palming my ass.

Rolling on my side, I dug around in the drawer of my nightstand, realizing that I still needed to put fresh batteries in my vibrator after it had abruptly died on me last time I used it.

Thankfully it let out a low, steady buzz when I switched it on.

Settling back against my pillows, head against the headboard, I closed my eyes and imagined Ford's face. The intensity of his eyes, the wickedness of his grin. I imagined his smiling mouth against mine, kissing me deeply, his tongue exploring my mouth. Getting more aggressive, moans coming from the back of his throat, showing me how much he wanted me.

I slipped the vibrator between my legs, letting it rest against the fabric of my underwear so we could both warm up. It didn't take much to push me over the edge, thanks to my lack of experience, so I tried to take it slow whenever possible. Draw it out. Remove all expectations and any sense of pressure, just letting myself coast.

He'd press me up against the wall—in my fantasy it was after hours at the country club and we were alone, the bar empty and quiet, just the two of us and the echo of our desperate breathing. Ford would have one hand wrapped around my ponytail, tugging firmly, sending little shocks of pleasure across my scalp.

His other hand would dip under my waistband, straight down the front of my panties, stroking me. I traced the tip of the vibrator up and down against the sensitive skin of my inner thighs, teasing myself until I had goosebumps, imagining it was Ford's fingers.

Then he'd slip his fingers inside my underwear, discovering my wet, swollen lips.

"You bad girl," he'd say. "You're already wet for me."

I pushed my underwear down and drew the vibrator slowly up my opening, letting it just barely rest against my clit, pretending it was Ford's thumb. Shivering, I slipped a finger inside my pussy, then two, my hips undulating as I imagined I was grinding against Ford's fingers.

In my bed, I let out a moan, stopping to adjust my position so I was facedown with the vibrator inside me. As I rode the gently pulsing silicone, I imagined us against the wall again, Ford still kissing me as my hands went for the zipper of his jeans. I could be bold in my fantasy, tugging his briefs down and taking his length in my hand. Giving it a squeeze.

Then I'd drop to my knees in front of him, wrapping my mouth around him and sucking softly, just enough to drive him crazy, then harder, until I tasted that first salty drop of precum.

"I have to fuck you," he'd say, desperate. "I need you. Please." And I'd nod.

As I squeezed my legs tighter around my vibrator, I imagined standing up, turning around, and spreading my legs. Ford would come up behind me to tear my underwear off and slip his thick cock inside, sheathing himself in me, filling me all the way up.

"How does this big cock feel inside that tight little pussy?" he'd ask.

"So good," I whispered, clicking the vibrator speed up another notch. "Fuck yes, Ford."

I bit my lip and closed my eyes, daydreaming about getting fucked, now with my palms pressed against the floor-to-ceiling windows at the club, my breath fogging the glass as Ford's grip tightened on my hips, his groans echoing in my ear as we found our rhythm. Me, thrusting my ass back, him, pumping into me harder. Faster. Deeper. I turned my toy up to max speed.

Facedown in my bed, I felt the waves of pleasure building up inside me, my orgasm rushing closer. I was right at the edge, my clit hot and swollen, my moans pitching higher. *Yes.* Spreading my legs as wide as I could, I let myself go, gasping Ford's name as I came in a hard rush, my whole body shuddering against the sheets, my vibrator wringing every last burst of pleasure from my body even as the battery finally gave out.

Spent and panting, I rolled over, staring up at the ceiling.

I was playing a very dangerous game indeed.

EMZEE

CHAPTER 6

Confession: I have a teeny tiny tendency to overthink things. And not just some things.
Everything.

This meant that beyond the endless analysis of all my personal and professional relationships, I was the kind of person who looked up menus online before going to new restaurants so I'd already have my order figured out, who spent two whole months researching flea medications before finally choosing one for Munchkin, and who showed up at least an hour early to every single photo shoot I got booked for.

For me, it was practical. I had to get a feel for the set. Scope everything out from top to bottom. Prepare a shot list in advance. I knew some photographers liked to be more "organic" and shoot on the fly, and of course I budgeted some time for that, but if I walked onto set exactly on time and tried to figure things out as I went? Disaster.

Still, I always enjoyed winding down toward the end of the shoot, when I was finished with all the photos I'd planned out and everyone could let their hair down and be more creative. The models could play in the space, I could experiment with lighting and composition. In fact, some of the strongest images in my portfolio were from these more informal sessions.

At the moment, though, I was concerned with staking out my set.

Or at least, that's what I was *trying* to do.

Problem was, ever since that day at the country club when Ford acted like we were already officially dating, I'd been kind of a mess. We hadn't talked about it yet, and he'd probably assumed I was too busy with work to return his calls, but I wondered if he even realized that I hadn't *actually* given him an answer about whether or not I'd help him out.

Thankfully, I could throw myself into my work. It would give me something more pressing and important to exert my energy on than Ford Malone.

I checked in with security when I stepped off the elevator and then walked onto the set, my favorite camera strapped around my neck, my hair pulled up in a sensible ponytail, and my ubiquitous boots laced up on my feet. First one there. Ready to rock.

For the shoot, Danica Rose had booked out the entire top floor bar at a fancy historic hotel in the affluent Gold Coast neighborhood. Through the wall of windows, Chicago's iconic skyline was on view in the distance. I'd play with the depth of field when I took the photos so the view wouldn't draw the eye away from the models. And I'd definitely want to take advantage of all the natural light coming in. I nodded as I paced the perimeter of the space, tapping notes to myself on my iPad.

Once I had a tentative shot list put together, I laid out the rest of my equipment on a long table. I'd been a fan of

Annie Leibovitz since forever and made it a point to work with a lot of the same cameras that she did. Including the one around my neck: the Nikon D810.

It was a gift I'd bought myself with the money from my first photography job that hadn't been handed to me via KZ Modeling. I'd done some of my best work with it.

Not recently, though. Ever since the trafficking scandal at KZM had blown up, my bookings had gotten fewer and far between. For a while, I worried the entire industry had decided to permanently blackball me, but once the media had started reporting more of the facts—namely, that my brothers and I verifiably had nothing to do with our father's crimes—the gigs had started trickling back in. Meanwhile, my brothers and I were still fighting to clean up the Zoric name.

But none of that would matter if the Bratva got ahold of us.

"Where do you want the fill light to go?" a member of the crew asked.

I looked over. "Hmmm...let's try on the other side of the bar."

By the time everything was set up and I had the lights positioned exactly where I wanted them, the first models were out of wardrobe and makeup and ready to get to work (not that I didn't consider the glamifying to be work in and of itself—it was).

Today we'd be shooting images to support the visual component of the Danica Rose rebrand. Gone were the days of the stilted black-and-white glamor shots that my father used to favor, where the models wore too much makeup and not enough clothes and sat around pouting in front of stark white walls or lounging on black granite stair-cases. Now, the agency was all about color, fresh faces, movement, diversity, and relaxed, natural poses and expressions.

I'd done a bunch of these shoots over the last few months, each one fun and different, all taking place at uniquely Chicago-centric locations like the Fleetwood Roller Rink and the Crystal Gardens at Navy Pier. The purpose of these shoots was twofold: first, to showcase our models to their best advantage for potential clients while helping keep their portfolios up to date, and second, to prove to the world that things at our agency were different now.

I hoped our efforts were working.

I didn't like to brag, but it had been me who stepped forward to suggest giving our agency a complete visual over-haul to go along with the new name.

It was a nice change, to be so involved. Treated like an equal. My father had been reluctant to allow me into the business in any way—getting hired as in-house photographer had been hard enough—and I hadn't ever dreamed I'd be responsible for more than that.

"Who wants music?" I asked, pitching my voice loud enough for everyone to hear.

The resounding answer from the models and the crew was a yes, so I plugged my phone into a set of good quality wireless speakers and cued up the playlist I'd put together to help set the mood. I did this for each of my shoots, tailoring the songs to the vibe I hoped to capture. Since today was all about fun, the playlist was a mix of upbeat, recent pop and classic rock.

As we started shooting, music blasting, people smiling and sometimes singing along, I realized that this was exactly what I needed right now. This was the perfect distraction from what had been going on between me and Ford.

For the next few hours, I was completely in the zone. The models were glowing and at ease, loving the "story" of the shoot—a Sunday brunch with friends, complete with piles of breakfast foods they were actually supposed to eat, that had to keep getting refreshed by the on-call wait staff every hour or so—and the classic gangster-glam atmosphere of the bar.

The energy on set was fantastic. I was glad my brothers had approved my idea, and that they'd also given me the go-ahead to hire an extra assistant whose sole purpose was to make sure the food also looked perfect in each shot. You rarely saw food involved in fashion photography; it was usually clothes, makeup, jewelry, shoes, bags, whatever. I knew this would catch the eye.

We kept our food assistant busy all morning. When Katya took a huge forkful of Chantilly cream-piled French toast so I could snap a photo with her biting into it, we had to replace the dish with a fresh one every few shots. And then she got some whipped cream on her nose and Jennika couldn't stop laughing, so I took a few photos of the giggle fest.

"You've all been amazing," I announced, clapping my hands, "so why don't we take a break? Fifteen or twenty, do what you need to do, then meet me back here."

Everyone drifted away, and I took a deep breath. I was getting the shots I wanted; I could feel it. Thank God the days of shooting flawless statues instead of real women were over.

I was in the midst of clicking through some of the digital shots I'd taken when I sensed a commotion behind me.

Nothing big, just some gossiping and giggles—but enough that I could hear it over the music. Break was just about over, but though the crew had started meandering back to set, my models seemed to have lost track of time. Which happened. No big deal. I'd go wrangle them.

But as I turned the corner around the wardrobe rack, I saw exactly what was causing the delay on my shoot.

Ford Malone. Eyes twinkling, dimples dimpling, his shirt sleeves rolled up to just exactly the right spot where his muscular forearms were gorgeously on display. Damn him.

I shouldn't have been surprised. The man loved models, after all.

And they loved him.

It was obvious he was flirting up a storm with all of my talent. And my hair and makeup techs. And my food fluffer. Clearly everyone was so drawn to his charisma, they'd completely forgotten they were supposed to be *at work*. I'd never seen so many batting eyelashes.

I wasn't surprised, but I *was* annoyed. Not at my people. At Ford. Shoots like this were my sanctuary—the one place I should have been safe from my obsession with him. Not today.

"I need everyone back to set now," I said, after clearing my throat loudly.

Ford lifted a hand in greeting, but I ignored it and turned to Katya, who was still staring at him with longing in her big blue eyes. Then he reached out to tuck a loose lock of hair behind her ear, and I felt my stomach clench.

"Katya! Now," I barked, making her jump a little. Then I turned my gaze to Ford, glaring at him. "I don't recall inviting you here."

Turning on my heel to go, I caught him smirking at my rebuke. God, he was infuriating. I wondered how he'd even found out where I was shooting today.

I took a few more pictures, but as much as I tried to get back in the groove, I soon had to admit that my mojo was gone. Things were feeling a bit too forced, the talent was acting less natural, and it seemed like the whole vibe had shifted. Probably due to that smoldering-hot faux-boyfriend of mine, watching intently from the side. Thankfully, I already had what I needed.

"We're done," I told Katya, releasing her. "Great work." Then I called wrap for everyone else and thanked them profusely for their time and energy, like I always did.

As the women disappeared to change and get on their way, I started packing up my equipment, purposefully ignoring Ford. But of course he strolled right over to me, all cocky-like.

"What the hell are you even doing here?" I snapped. I had the right. It was my work place, after all. And he hadn't told me he was coming, nor had I invited him.

If my attitude bothered Ford, he didn't show it. Instead, he just grinned at me. That stupid, handsome, perfect grin that made me forget what I was even pissed about to begin with.

"I came to take you to dinner," he said. "Please tell me you're free."

He had always been charming, but I'd rarely had that charm directed so completely at me and me alone. It was unnerving. I couldn't resist it.

Even knowing full well that this was all pretend, that he never would have stopped by out of the blue if we weren't involved in these fake dating shenanigans. But who cared what the reason was? He was here, and he wanted to take me out.

"I'm not dressed for dinner," I said, gesturing at my ripped-knee jeans and combat boots.

"Then we'll make a quick stop at your place. I'll walk

Munch while you get ready," Ford said, taking my hand. "Say yes."

Sparks spread up my arm instantly, and I wondered if he could feel my pulse racing.

Trying to act nonchalant, and fighting off the warm fuzzies that I got whenever Ford used his nickname for my dog, I said, "Yeah, I guess I could make it work. But look, you really can't be flirting with other people if we're going to sell this. You had those models eating out of your hand, and half my crew to boot. Next time, try to act like you're not interested."

His smile grew—and this time my knees really did go weak. And other parts of me seemed to be waking up. I flushed as I remembered what I'd done, alone in my bedroom, the extended fantasy I'd played out about our last interaction.

"See? I knew you were gonna be my girlfriend," he said.

God help me.

EMZEE

CHAPTER 7

One thing I'd been groomed for from a very young age was how to be a good dinner party guest. Which, it turned out, was really going to save my bacon—because as it happened, I'd need every ounce of poise and manners and all those lists of innocuous discussion topics at my disposal to get through my first Official Girlfriend Event: dinner with the Malones.

When I was younger, I had resented all the drills and etiquette lessons. I hadn't wanted to learn poise and manners and how to make small talk with rich, snobby people. I'd wanted to take more photography lessons and study art history and go outside and take pictures.

But my father had insisted, and so I'd learned exactly which forks to use with which courses during a meal. I'd learned how to dress for certain events, how to style my hair to look respectable, how to do my makeup so I looked reasonably put together and not totally trampy. In essence, I'd learned how to be a lady.

Usually, I ignored all that shit. I had my black boots, my black eyeliner, and my attitude.

Tonight, though? I was glad to be able to fall back on my training.

When Ford had said he was taking me to dinner, I'd naïvely assumed that it would be a private dinner out, just the two of us. A chance to talk about this plan of his in more detail.

Instead, after we'd gone back to my apartment, after he'd fed and walked my dog while I put on a little black dress and actual heels, worked some product into my hair and put on a dash of makeup, he'd called a private car to drop us off at a very nice restaurant in a very nice hotel.

Where his entire family was waiting.

"You didn't tell me we were having dinner with your family," I hissed at him once I realized what was happening.

"Didn't I?" he asked, looking completely nonplussed.

I glared at him in response, and he just grinned back.

"Relax. It's just my family. And a few of their business associates," he said.

A few? That was an understatement. Being Who They Were, the Malones had taken over the entirety of the Travelle Restaurant at the Langham Hotel to entertain in style, and the place was filled to the brim with people. Most of whom I'd never met before.

"You'll be fine," Ford said, taking my coat. "I'll be right next to you all night."

"Right. Just like you were 'right next to me all night' at your mom's party?"

Eyes focusing on something over my shoulder, Ford murmured, "Speak of the devil..." and then louder, "Mother!"

Turning me around, he dragged me over to his mom. She was dressed head to toe in silver sequins, and as ridiculous as that might sound, she somehow looked very nice.

Her eyes lit up. "Ford, darling, you made it." She glanced at me, and it was clear from her expression that she was just as displeased by my presence as I was to be there. "And Mara."

"Mrs. Malone. You look well," I forced myself to say, smiling politely. It was going to be a long night.

Thankfully, there was a room full of people between us.

I quickly ascertained that most of the guests were Malone Real Estate Holdings employees and business associates, and that's when it really hit me: Ford hadn't asked me out to dinner so we could sort out his half-baked fake girlfriend plan. This was the equivalent of tossing someone into the deep end of the pool and hoping they'd figure out how to swim.

This was our official coming out as a couple. Holy hell.

"Are you ready?" Ford asked me, putting his arm around my waist.

"I was born ready," I answered, already turning on my bubbly party persona full force.

Ford grinned down at me. "You're the best, Em," he said. "I really owe you one."

And there it was. That delicious, dimpled smile. The genuine gratitude. Drat.

We began making our way through the crowd. I knew we'd end up at his parents' table eventually, but Ford seemed content to take his time, talking at length to everyone we passed.

Admittedly, I got a thrill every single time he introduced me as his girlfriend. It made it a lot easier to smile and shake hands and occasionally exchange those airy cheek-kisses with everyone I met. The funny part was, I didn't actually know much about real estate—so all the shop talk Ford engaged in with people was interesting enough that I had no trouble paying attention and asking appropriate questions. It was night and day compared to the locker room talk I'd witnessed between Ford and his colleagues that day at the country club.

Finally, we made it to the head table, where Ford's mother ignored me and his father gave me a neutral smile. Mr. Malone had always seemed like a textbook workaholic to me—Ford rarely talked about him now, and I knew he'd been largely absent during Ford's youth.

"This is Emzee, remember?" Ford reminded him, kissing the top of my head and sending warmth all the way down to my toes. "My brilliant photographer friend. We're dating now."

"Ah. Excellent," Mr. Malone said. He was probably in his sixties, but he was devilishly handsome, with deep dimples and an air of easy charm—it was obvious where Ford got those things from. "Welcome to the fold, Emzee."

I could feel myself blushing as I let him take my hand and give it a warm, gentlemanly shake. It almost made me sad to be lying to the man about my relationship with Ford.

Then we took our seats and dinner began. As expected, even the first course of amuse-bouche was a feast for the eyes and the mouth, an artistic arrangement of endives with triple-cream Brie and rhubarb compote. Then came the soup, a featherlight cream of asparagus topped with shaved chives and crème fraîche. I was shocked at how much I didn't hate it.

"Got yourself a new girl, eh?" the older man across from us asked.

He was talking to Ford, but his eyes were focused on my cleavage.

"Yes, this is my girlfriend, Mara," Ford said, not seeming to notice that I was getting ogled. Still, I appreciated him using my full name with this stranger. It made me feel seen, the way that Ford intuitively understood that my nickname wasn't fair game for just anyone to know and use. "We've known each other since our days at the Academy."

"Ah," the older man said. "Young love."

"Mara, this is Nathan Watson, a very accomplished and well-regarded developer," Ford went on by way of introduction. "We share a box with his family at the Chicago Symphony."

I had a hard time imagining any of Ford's family members attending the symphony for the music. They probably just went to be seen. I wondered if Mr. Watson did the same.

"Do you like the symphony, my dear?" he asked, his gaze still fixed on my chest.

I shifted in my seat, politely ignoring his staring while subtly adjusting the strap of my dress in order to better cover myself. The dress wasn't even that low-cut, honestly, but with boobs like mine, there was always the danger of spillage. Moments like these, I dreamed of having an A cup, or even a small B. A girl could dream.

"I do," I said. "The new season looks wonderful. I actually can't wait for the Beethoven festival. It's his two-hundred-fiftieth birthday this year, you know."

Mr. Watson nodded. "Did you catch the Sibelius and Nielsen last year? It was divine."

By the time the salad arrived, he had moved on from our conversation and refocused his attention on the gentleman seated to his right, who wanted to discuss stock portfolios.

The man on his left, however, looked down into his

fennel salad and inexplicably turned to his dining companion, a woman in a sharp, bespoke suit—likely one of the MREH investors.

"Remind me to offload some cash before the end of the fiscal quarter," he said to her. "Taxes are such a killjoy when you can't stop making money."

They both laughed.

I cleared my throat, gently. Respectfully. Readjusted my dress again.

"Excuse me for interrupting, but if you're in the process of researching tax deductible options," I said, keeping my voice sweet, "I actually chair a wonderful charity that can always benefit from the support of generous individuals. We're also happy to include your contact information on our website, which can help drive additional business interests your way. Not that you need it, from the sound of things."

"I'm intrigued," the woman said immediately, leaning in. "Can you tell me more?"

Soon enough, I'd secured their commitment to sponsoring two year-long classes for my charity. At the very least, I could leave this dinner feeling like I'd accomplished something beyond helping Ford distract his mother from his dating life.

Ford's Aunt Miri—an older woman who I had noticed was wearing a wristful of studded bracelets with an edge to them—turned to me during the fish course to comment on my purse.

"It's so chic," she said. "I just adore Prada."

"It's from the new collection." I passed it over so she could examine it. "I'm not one to buy a new bag every season, but this one's a classic. It's Saffiano leather."

"It is exquisite," she said, stroking the handstitched leather before handing it back. "I love a piece that transcends time. You'll have this forever, dear."

"I think so, too. This style won't be out for a few more weeks, but I have a hookup through work," I said. "If you're interested, I'd be happy to pull those strings again."

She seemed delighted and I smiled. It was the first fun conversation I'd had all evening, and we chatted about the punk aesthetic of Alexander McQueen and Vivienne Westwood through the rest of the meal. So far, she was the nicest member of Ford's family I'd met that evening. And I appreciated the fact that she wasn't staring at me like I was toilet paper on the bottom of someone's shoe, the way Ford's mother was whenever I caught her looking my way.

I knew it was only a matter of time before she said something.

She waited until dessert was served.

It was a perfect, golden, featherlight lemon soufflé that had me practically moaning at the first bite. My pleasure must have been evident, because Ford's dad commented from his seat at the end of the table that it looked like I was enjoying myself.

Blushing, I admitted that it was the best soufflé I'd ever had, which was saying something since I was a bit of a connoisseur. Before he could respond, Mrs. Malone chimed in with, "You know I must admit, Emzee, I was so *very* surprised to see that you, of all people, had caught my son's eye."

"Really," I said, trying to keep my tone light. "I guess it goes to show, you never know."

"In my experience, it's not always about falling in love at first sight," Mr. Malone said with a warm smile. "Sometimes you have to look again."

Despite Mr. Malone's kinder words, Ford must have sensed me tensing up beside him. A thrill went up my spine as he linked our fingers together. Even though I knew he was probably just doing it for the benefit of all the eyes on us, I still relished the contact.

His mother, however, couldn't keep her mouth shut.

"After all these years," she went on grandly, "we really just thought of you as a piece of the furniture."

Her words felt like a slap across the face. I wasn't sure what to do or say, frozen in my seat with that stupid fake smile on, my cheeks burning with humiliation, squeezing Ford's hand.

And on she went, "I can't imagine what suddenly changed my son's mind out of the blue, especially when he and—"

"Mother," Ford cut her off, a warning edge to his voice. Her voice was loud enough that several heads were turning in our direction now.

"Oh Ford, dear, do calm down," she said, pausing only long enough to sip her wine. "I'm simply saying we were so used to seeing her in the background all the time...following you around like a little shadow..."

She was making it seem like I was some pathetic little thing that had shown up in their lives one day and then refused to leave. My face had grown even hotter—everyone was staring at us now—and I wanted to sink under the table and crawl away.

As if he could sense my desire to run, Ford's hand tightened around mine.

"Mother, stop," he said, his voice quiet.

But she didn't.

"She's just so quiet and unassuming, not your usual

type at all," she said, taking another drink of wine. She was obviously tipsy. "More like a mouse, really."

She laughed at that, and the friends sitting around her laughed as well.

Okay. Enough. Time to go.

I started to push my chair back, but clearly Ford had other ideas.

He let go of my hand and wrapped his arm around my shoulders, pulling me close. I didn't realize what was happening until it was too late, until his other hand was warm and gentle on my chin, tilting my face toward his. I didn't have time to prepare. I didn't have time to do anything, really. My body knew what was coming, though, and my eyes closed instinctively as his mouth pressed against mine. Hot, firm, and just a little bit wet.

Sweet Jesus.

I'd dreamed about kissing Ford ever since I was sixteen. I'd fantasized about it happening a million times, in a million different ways. But I'd never imagined it would happen in public, in a crowded restaurant, surrounded by his family and business associates.

This was our first kiss. In front of unfriendly eyes, yes, but so soft and sweet and reassuring that for a second it made everything else melt away. For a moment, I completely lost myself in the feel of Ford's arms around me, his lips on mine.

For a moment, it was perfect.

My entire body buzzed with the pleasure of his touch. The kiss was chaste, as far as kisses went, but I felt it everywhere. Especially between my legs.

And then I heard his mother's gasp, snapping me back to reality.

"Come now, Ford," she scolded as we pulled apart. "No need to be vulgar."

"There's nothing vulgar about kissing my girl," he said, cupping my cheek. My heart was still pounding in my chest. I couldn't tear my eyes away from his.

The kiss was everything I'd ever dreamed of.

And that was exactly why I had to break this off.

EMZEE

CHAPTER 8

After that kiss, the rest of the evening passed in a blur.

We said our fond farewells and got out of the restaurant without further incident, but as I waited for my Uber to pull up outside the hotel, Ford decided to make a big show out of saying goodbye to me.

Everyone else was trickling out the doors as well, waiting for their own cars to come back from the valet lot, or for private car services to roll up. We had quite an audience.

"I appreciate you coming out tonight," he said rather loudly, pulling me close and looking down into my eyes. "It really meant a lot to me and my family."

"Um, you're welcome?" I didn't think he could possibly be serious, because this definitely wasn't how he usually spoke to me. "Thanks for having me."

"No," he said, his hands tightening on my hips. "Thank *you*."

"Ford, please. Your Town Car will be here any moment," his mother said from behind him. "Come and wait with the rest of us."

I frowned, but it barely had a chance to form on my lips before Ford was kissing me again. It was different this time, because unlike that first kiss, we were standing...which meant the full length of our bodies were pressed right up against each other.

God, he felt good. Solid, strong, warm. He added a hint more of his tongue this time and it made my head swim. I melted into his arms, unable to help myself.

These kisses were going to be the death of me.

I heard Ford's mother make a huff of annoyance, but I didn't care.

Without warning, Ford suddenly let go and stepped back. He had a smug, self-satisfied look on his face and I deflated, realizing I'd gotten carried away—that he merely considered that goodbye kiss to be Mission Accomplished.

Just then, my phone buzzed with a text: my car had arrived. It pulled up to the curb beside the Rideshare App sign and the driver's side window rolled down.

"Uber for Mara," he said. As if there was any doubt that the one banged-up silver Toyota sedan in a sea of sleek black Town Cars and valeted luxury vehicles could be for anyone but me.

"Yes, that's me," I said with a sigh, adjusting the purse over my shoulder.

Ford opened the door for me and gestured for me to get in the back seat, but on impulse I turned back and grabbed his hand, saying, "Drive home with me."

It was kind of brilliant on my part. Because we had an audience—with his parents and all their business associates standing around watching us, I knew Ford couldn't question my motives. I had him. Though I was sure he assumed I was just playing along with the whole charade, really giving it my all.

And that was fine with me. If he could manipulate our friendship to make me agree to participate in this whole thing, then I could manipulate his lie to suit my own purposes as well.

Because we really, really needed to talk through this fake dating stuff. I couldn't keep getting blindsided by surprise dinners where I got unexpectedly kissed every time his mother said something rude. I needed to lay some ground rules. Set some boundaries.

"I'll cancel my car," he announced loudly, obviously for the benefit of everyone nearby.

It was clear what this must have looked like. Especially after that public kiss. I was the smitten girlfriend dying to have her boyfriend all to herself. And Ford, for his part, was the boyfriend who was just as excited to be going home with his girlfriend.

He climbed into the back seat after me, with a hungry expression that almost said he hoped this would turn out to be something other than what it was—a show. Was it possible that he thought this was real? That I was actually dragging him home for a booty call, as if we were a real couple? And why did that thought make my skin tingle so hard with anticipation?

It took less than a minute to realize that whatever I'd thought Ford was feeling in the moment was actually just more of the same act he'd been putting on throughout dinner. Because as soon as we pulled away, he pulled his phone out to set up his own ride home from my loft.

"That was a nice touch," he said, grinning. "My mother is going to have her pantyhose twisted all night realizing how serious we are to be going home together."

He gave me a brief, approving look.

"Good thinking," he said. "My driver will meet me at your place."

A flash of annoyance washed over me.

"Actually, that wasn't why I wanted you to come with me," I said. "We need to talk."

Turning my way, he put his phone back in his pocket and gave me his full attention. For the first time since this whole thing had started, I finally felt like he was focused solely on me.

It made my heart flutter.

I wondered what he would do if I told him something completely different than what I had intended. For the briefest moment, I let myself imagine a scenario where I confessed my true feelings. How would he react? Would he take me in his arms and kiss me again, admitting he'd always secretly felt the same? Ha. More likely he'd open the car door and roll out onto the street rather than be alone with me and my pathetic emotions. I'd probably never hear from him again.

Still, I desperately hoped for option number one. The fantasy was so alive and vivid in my mind that I couldn't quite come out and say what I wanted to say.

Instead, I danced around it. "You're my best friend," I told him. "You know that, right?"

"Sure. Why? What's going on?" Ford asked, his eyes searching mine.

I took a deep breath, trying to stay focused. "Am I...*your* best friend?"

I didn't know exactly what I was hoping for, or what I was expecting him to say. But his shoulders relaxed and that classic dimpled Ford grin spread across his lips, filling me with warmth as he said, "Of course." Then he laughed. "I have *all* the friend feelings for you. I love you as much as I'd love a sibling. If I had one. I'm sure of it."

Ugh. Just like that, the warmth I'd felt was gone. I was instantly deflated, my childish fantasy of him taking me into his arms fading completely.

It was time to end this now, before it went any further. It wasn't fair. To him, or to me.

Glancing out the window, I tried to steel myself. Gather my strength and willpower.

"Look," I told him. "I've done as much as I can, but I can't go along with this anymore. It's too much lying, and at this point, I've had enough lies to last a lifetime. You know?"

I watched his face, trying to gauge his reaction.

If anything, Ford should be able to understand exactly what I meant. After all, he was the one who'd gotten me through all the stress of finding out my dad had been using KZ Modeling as a cover for his sex trafficking ring. He knew what the stress had done to me, what the lies had cost my family. What it had cost me. And it was no secret that I still wasn't over the whole thing.

"I get what you're saying," he said softly.

"Good. Because I need to be honest with my family," I said. "And you need to be honest with yours. Just remind them that your personal life is your business, and say you need some time to yourself." He was nodding as I spoke, which was encouraging. I took a deep breath. "I think it's time to break up."

He stopped nodding and looked out the window, not saying anything for a moment.

"Things were going so well," he finally murmured.

"For you, yes," I said, trying not to sound accusatory. "This isn't great for me, though."

That seemed to get through to him. "You sure about this?" he said.

"Yeah. I'm sure."

"Okay. You're right. It's time."

It broke my heart a little that he didn't push more, but I knew I'd made the right choice. In fact, the way he was willing to let me go so soon and so easily was proof enough that our faux relationship would have only led to harder heartbreak for me.

"Would it be okay if we told everyone at the Investment Ball this weekend?" he asked, turning those pleading eyes on me. "You're still planning to go to that, right?"

"Of course I'll be there," I said. "I can wait until then."

I'd already promised to go, and I wasn't the kind of person who broke my promises. Besides, Ford and I were still friends. Even if we hadn't been fake dating, I would have been attending as his plus-one now that Claudia was permanently out of the picture.

Letting out a long breath, I tried to shake off the tension I'd been carrying around all week. Finally, things could go back to normal between us. But mixed with the relief was a heavy dose of disappointment.

This was the most time that Ford and I had spent together in forever, and even though it was all because of his ruse, I could admit there were parts of it that I had enjoyed.

Like the kisses.

No. I had to push those memories out of my head, banish them for good. The whole point of ending this was so I could get over my crush on Ford, not tend it like a sacred flame. I needed to go back to my original plan—put myself out there, start dating for real, and see if I could find a compatible someone who had their shit together and actually wanted to be with me.

We pulled up to my building, where Ford's driver was already waiting.

"Looks like your ride's here," I told him, reaching for the door handle. "See you."

I expected him to head to his Town Car immediately and leave, but instead he waited for me to get out of the car and then walked me up to the doors of my building, his hand on my lower back the whole time.

I tried not to read too much into it. Especially when his gaze dropped down to my lips for half a second. But before I could think about it too much, he pulled me into a good night hug. A friendly, "I love you as much as I'd love a sibling" type hug that only reinforced that I'd made the right choice.

"Thanks for playing along while you could," he said. "I really appreciate it."

"Sure," I said. "No problem. It was fun."

At least only half of that was a lie.

"I'll call you," he said, just like he always did. Guess we really were back to normal.

I headed into the lobby of my building, turning once I got to the elevator to wave at Ford who was still waiting outside. As I watched, he headed to his car, got in the back seat, and then disappeared into the night. It was all over now.

Somehow, I managed to get all the way up to the top floor and inside my loft before the tears began to fall.

I sank to the floor, Munchkin in my lap, sobbing like my heart was breaking.

It wasn't fair. The whole thing with Ford had been fake all along. So why did this breakup feel so much like the real thing?

EMZEE

CHAPTER 9

I couldn't have picked a better setting for ending my fake relationship with Ford than the Investment Ball. Heads had turned the moment we entered the ballroom, and the first person we'd run into was his delightful Aunt Miri, with whom I'd chatted during the dinner at Travelle.

"You're glowing," she had said to me. "I'm so glad you both could make it." Then she fawned over my dress, complimenting my style so much that I blushed.

Part of the reason I was "glowing" was because of the attention Ford was giving me. Even knowing that this was going to be the end of our charade, that we'd soon go back to being just friends, that this night would be the last time I'd feel the warmth of his hand in mine.

We mingled for a few more minutes, and everyone was pleasant. I had to admit, the event was already going better than I'd anticipated. Ford looked beyond GQ-handsome in his perfectly tailored tux, and for once, I felt evenly matched in my brand-new gown. Considering that this was going to be our last night out together as a "couple," I'd gone all out, begging my contact at Prada to express mail me one of their latest designs in my exact measurements. It fit like a dream. I felt like one of the models I'd spent my whole life around.

Minus the whole height thing.

It didn't make sense that I'd ended up so pocket-sized, given that both of my parents were tall. Almost as though all the height in our family had already been distributed to Stefan and Luka before I was even born. But despite it bothering me when I was little, I had to admit that after getting picked on in school, I'd developed a distinct appreciation for being able to blend in a little more easily. To fold in on myself and become invisible when necessary.

But tonight, in this dress, in these heels (also new), Ford couldn't stop staring at me. And as I sipped a flute of champagne, I was happy to bask in the attention. After all, Cinderella had enjoyed the ball right up until the magic ran out at midnight, too. There was no point in wasting all these dances and drinks anticipating anything other than the joy of whirling around the floor in the arms of Ford Malone.

Tonight, I was going to savor every moment we had together. I wasn't going to think about tomorrow, when we'd be back to business as usual.

This was my chance to live the dream.

Ford was the perfect date. My champagne glass was never empty, my hand always clasped in his. We danced almost every dance together, and he made me feel like I was the center of his world.

"You are killing it in this dress," he whispered in my ear as we spun across the dance floor, trailing his fingers up and down my spine until I shivered.

The back of my gown was open and cut low, almost obscenely so, and apparently the bare skin of my back was too enticing for Ford to keep his hands off it. Which I didn't exactly mind, even though I was far more exposed than I'd usually be comfortable with. But something about this outfit tonight made me feel powerful and confident. Maybe it was the dress, or the fuck-me heels, or having Ford as an accessory on my arm. Probably all of the above.

I didn't want it to end.

But I knew that it had to.

It was nearing midnight when I noticed Ford's parents making their overtures to leave. Ford's father hovered near Mrs. Malone, making little tutting noises while she said her lengthy goodbyes. Mrs. Malone could hold him off for a few more minutes, but not much longer.

I could tell that Ford had noticed as well, judging by the way he stiffened in my arms. We were waltzing when it happened, so I sensed that once the song was over, so was the fairy tale.

We couldn't put it off any longer.

The song ended, and Ford squared his shoulders and took a deep breath. Even though I'd basically been a puddle of longing all night, it made me melt a little more. I knew this couldn't be easy for him.

As much as I'd been frustrated with Ford's decision to lie to his parents, I understood it. He hated disappointing them; he thought the responsibility of his family's happiness was on his shoulders. It had always been that way. Not that he'd ever directly told me that, and maybe he didn't even admit it to himself, but we'd been friends for seven years and I knew I wasn't wrong. It had always been clear to me that he had that magical thinking of so many children of unhappily married parents—that if he was just good enough, he could somehow fix them.

As we crossed the room toward the Malones, I wished I

could pull him to the side and tell him he was enough. That nothing he did could ever change how his parents treated each other—or how they treated him—but that life shouldn't be about trying to live up to the expectations of other people. Maybe that was a conversation for another day.

Hand in hand, we reached Ford's parents. His mother's eyes lit up at the sight of him, but that excitement quickly dimmed when her gaze turned toward me.

"Oh, Emzee," she said dourly. "I didn't realize you were still here."

"Mother—" Ford warned.

"We were just about to leave," Mr. Malone cut in. "Good to see you again, Emzee. I hope you'll have a pleasant remainder of the evening."

"Do we really have to go so soon?" his mother whined.

"Actually," Ford said, interrupting them, "I'm glad I caught you before you head out. I wanted to speak to you about—"

"Caught us!" his mother scoffed. "You've been ignoring us all evening. I don't think I've ever seen you dance at one of these events before, and now all of a sudden you're Fred Astaire."

I didn't say anything, just gave Ford's hand a squeeze. Encouraging him. But before he could get another word out, his father was looking past both of us.

"Ah, Claudia," he said. "We were wondering if we'd see you tonight."

My stomach dropped, and Ford's grip suddenly tightened on mine.

Adrenaline kicking, we turned around to find Ford's ex-girlfriend standing there, looking absolutely radiant as always. Tall, blonde, blue-eyed, and flawlessly, haughtily gorgeous. In fact, even though we were both wearing black dresses and heels, her ensemble somehow made my brand new Prada outfit feel downright shabby. Maybe it was Claudia's height; I always felt like I shrank down to nothing when I stood next to her.

Not only that, but without actually uttering a single unkind word, she always managed to make me feel just like I did as the high school whore everyone hated. Out of place and unwanted.

"Claudia," Ford's mother crooned, her expression softening as she pulled Claudia in for a hug. "It's so good to see you. You're an absolute vision in that gown. The belle of the ball."

"Thank you, Mrs. Malone," Claudia said, her voice sickly sweet. "And you look stunning, as always. I'm so sorry to have missed your fête. I heard it was quite an affair."

I mean seriously, who called a birthday party a "fête"? Claudia, that's who.

Ford's mother preened, but I could tell her smile was genuine. "How kind of you to say so, my dear. You were sorely missed."

Just like the old days, both of them were standing inches away and yet completely ignoring me. Treating me like I was, well, a piece of the furniture. I gritted my teeth, still wearing my perfect party guest smile.

The worst part was that Claudia did look like the belle of the ball. Her dress plunged down to her sternum in the front, but the cut was so narrow that you only got the barest hint of cleavage. Classy. Her hair fell in silky waves to her shoulders, a lock falling artfully into her eyes, and her lips were siren red. She looked like one of those glamorous Hollywood starlets from the 1940s. Her lashes had to be a foot long, and she kept batting them in Ford's direction.

Our differences were once again thrown into high relief.

Claudia obviously wanted to be seen and was comfortable shining in the spotlight. I just wanted to hide. If this was the kind of woman that Ford liked, it was beyond stupid to think that I'd ever had a chance at capturing his heart, let alone his libido.

I wanted nothing more than to run out of there, but Ford was still holding my hand.

"I wasn't sure about the dress," Claudia was saying, turning right and left with her hands on her hips to show off the swish of the voluminous skirt. "I thought it might be too much."

"Oh never," Ford's mother said. "It's just right for black tie."

"What do you think?" Claudia turned toward us, still ignoring me. "Do you like it, Ford?"

She put a hand on his arm. I suppressed a growl. Ford didn't answer.

"Oh! Hello, Emzee," Claudia said, finally acknowledging me. "I didn't see you there. You look...very nice. It's so cute you two are here together."

I felt another growl building. Claudia always reminded me of a mannequin, so put together that it seemed very possible she had been created in an atelier rather than being born like a normal baby in a hospital. I hated how easily she could make my beautiful couture dress seem common and cheap. How easily she could make *me*—and my relationship, fake though it might be—feel common and cheap.

Ford cleared his throat. "We were just about to have a word with my parents," he said to Claudia. "So if you wouldn't mind excusing us for a few moments..."

Before Claudia could take the hint and sashay off to sparkle at someone else, Ford's mother put a protective hand on Claudia's arm and said, "That's right. What were you and Emzee about to tell us, dear?"

I wished we didn't have to do this in front of Claudia. I knew she would consider it a personal victory to know that Ford and I weren't together anymore. That our relationship had barely lasted a week.

But I also knew it had to be done. We couldn't keep pretending this way.

"What is it?" Mr. Malone asked, pointedly checking the time on his Breitling watch.

I couldn't blame him. He didn't seem all that interested in spending time with Claudia, either.

Ford gave my hand a squeeze and I smiled reassuringly up at him.

"Emzee and I had a long discussion..." he started.

"A discussion?" Claudia echoed.

"And?" Mr. Malone prodded.

"Yes?" his mother asked.

"And, uh—we're getting married!" Ford said. "Surprise!"

Their jaws collectively dropped to the floor. Meanwhile, my good party guest smile was frozen on my face.

Surprise? No one, and I mean no one, was more surprised than me.

EMZEE

CHAPTER 10

ord pulled me in close, his arm wrapped tight around me while he just kept on running that liar mouth of his.

"We wanted to wait for a more intimate setting to share the news, but we're just too excited. Aren't we, Em?"

I didn't know what to do. This was not the plan we'd gone over—not even close.

Somehow, I managed a nod.

"Uh-huh," I said.

I watched as the news sank in. Mr. Malone looked mildly surprised, but he certainly wasn't scowling. Ford's mother and Claudia, on the other hand...

"*What?*" Claudia said.

The smile had slid right off her face and she was staring at us, her jaw slack.

I couldn't really blame her. I was just as shocked as she was.

"You can't be serious, Ford darling," his mother was saying, literally clutching her pearls and forcing me to hold back a snicker.

"I know, it seems sudden," Ford said, dropping a quick kiss on the top of my head. "But then again, we've been friends for so long, I guess it just clicked for us all at once. How happy we are together."

"Well congratulations," Mr. Malone said, giving Ford a firm handshake.

"But Ford," Mrs. Malone started, but he didn't let her get another word in.

"No, Mother, we haven't set a date yet—I know that's what you were about to ask."

Ford had the biggest smile on his face, so I tried to focus on that as my thoughts spun out of control. How in the hell did we go from deciding to tell his parents that we weren't together to claiming that we were newly engaged? Just how far was Ford going to take this whole thing? Was he really that obsessed with proving to his mother that his relationship with Claudia was over, or was it Claudia's presence itself that was the catalyst for this new twist?

Every sentence he spoke just dug us deeper into the hole he had created, and all I could do was grin through my clenched jaw and nod along.

"We don't have a ring yet," Ford went on. "I was hoping to get Grandma's. It's not just the sentimental value; Emzee's really into vintage. It's perfect for her."

Well. That was the cherry on top of this whole ridiculous cake. Yes, I liked vintage, but his great-grandmother's fabled *heirloom diamond ring*? Ford's mother had never worn it herself, instead keeping it tucked away in a jewelry box for her only son to propose with—she'd been talking it up to him ever since he was a kid. I'd heard about it from Ford, had even seen the ring myself once, though lately the talk had been about Claudia's plans to take out the diamonds and use them as a halo for her dream engagement ring. Ford had been horrified at the suggestion.

In my opinion, the ring was perfect just the way it was. It was a Victorian piece in warm yellow gold, and had been custom designed with a double row of antique diamonds that had been passed down by prior Malone generations. Dainty, yes, but enduringly classic.

And yeah, it *was* perfect for me.

I'd always thought it was far too subtle an engagement ring for someone like Claudia—she wasn't into simplicity. She was the type of girl who'd only be happy with a huge, flawless, brilliant cut solitaire in a Tiffany setting, probably in platinum.

His mother's face was deceptively stoic now. I knew part of it was the Botox, but beyond that, she was probably in complete shock. And although I'd never interacted much with Mr. Malone, he was a very successful businessman, which meant he had long ago perfected his poker face. He was using it to great effect now. I couldn't tell what he was thinking.

I tried to find some inspiration for how to hide my horror by studying how well his parents presented their inscrutable expressions.

Later, though? I was going to kill Ford. I was going to truly, actually murder him.

"We'll have to talk about the ring later," Mrs. Malone said. "When it's...quieter."

"But we *will* talk about it," Ford pushed.

Even knowing full well this was all bullshit, I was also really enjoying making Ford's mother sweat the way she was. And the look on Claudia's face was priceless. She was visibly seething with jealousy, doing this little twitch thing she probably wasn't even aware of. After all those years of making me feel like I didn't matter, like I wasn't worthy of Ford's precious time and attention, the tables had turned.

No wonder Ford was so into this scheme. It was super fun.

I relaxed into Ford's embrace and let a real smile play across my lips. Yes, I was still pissed at him. But I could at least bask in the moment, couldn't I?

Already, I could hear people whispering around us. It was a little crazy how fast the news seemed to be spreading around the event already. There was no stopping it now. By the end of the evening, everyone here would know that Ford and I were engaged.

God only knew how long it would take to spread across the rest of Chicago...

The mess we had created had just gotten a whole lot bigger. There would be a lot of cleanup to do after tonight. But for now, I was just going to enjoy the sour look on Claudia's face and accept the well wishes of the people who had gathered, hoping to get in good with us.

"You have the makings of a real power couple," someone said.

"So good to see young people coming together when they're both so committed to making a difference," another chimed in.

Every time we turned, there was a new person waiting to congratulate us.

Everything was happening so fast, I could barely process any of it. My romantic, final night as Ford's fake girlfriend had turned into a makeshift celebration of our fake engagement. We were really in it now.

It was at least another hour before there was a chance for Ford and me to talk privately. The well-wishers had dwindled down, his parents were long gone, and poor

Claudia had suddenly gotten a "migraine" and had to leave soon after. Somehow, we were able to slip away from the ballroom and maneuver ourselves into a quiet corner.

I turned to Ford, fully intending to unleash my wrath on him. As he deserved.

But before I could, he had his hands up, almost as if he was waving a white flag.

"I know, I know," he said before I was even able to open my mouth. "Just hear me out."

I glared at him, crossing my arms. "You have exactly thirty seconds."

"I didn't plan this," Ford said.

"Really." I raised an eyebrow.

"I swear I didn't," he insisted. "It just happened. But honestly, the whole thing could really be a win/win."

Shaking my head, I laughed. "What could I possibly get out of this?"

Ford took my hand, his mischievous grin shifting to a more serious look. "Your family is still dealing with the fallout from what happened with your dad, right?" he asked.

"You want that kind of scandal rubbing off on you?" I asked. It didn't make any sense. "Trust me, you don't. If you're trying to piss off your mom, you're going about it all wrong."

"That's not what this is about," he said. "Imagine it: A blissful wedding between the youngest Zoric and the successful son of one of the most respected families in Chicago. The last hint of any possible scandal will be gone from your family for good."

As much as I hated to admit it, "You have a point."

"Your family will be thrilled, mine will be happy," Ford added.

"Not according to your mother's face they won't be," I said.

He took my other hand and pulled me closer, so we were standing face-to-face. I looked up at him, still skeptical.

"She just needs time to adjust," he said. "Trust me, she's been dreaming about me getting married since I was in diapers. This will be the crowning social event of her life. She'll love it."

"Ford, stop. You can't be suggesting we actually go through with this!"

"Why not? We can even make it official. Like with a contract."

"A contract?" I echoed. Pretending to be Ford's girlfriend was bad enough. Pretending to be his fiancée was even worse. A pretend marriage? That was a whole new world of bad ideas.

He was nodding, eyes lighting up as he got more and more excited by the idea. "We'll just fake it for a year, maybe. It has its benefits, Em. Focus on the benefits!"

I couldn't focus on anything while I was having such a hard time breathing.

Finally picking up on the fact that I wasn't saying very much, he let go of my hands and brought his up to cradle my face gently.

"Look," he said, his voice soft. "We both know what will happen if we don't do this. I'll bow to my mom's iron will and get back together with Claudia. We'll get married, because that's what everyone will expect us to do, and then spend the rest of my life miserable with her and our two point five clone children. And probably some purebred designer poodle named Winston."

"Claudia's allergic to dogs," I reminded him. "Maybe you could get a goldfish."

"Even worse," he said, cracking a smile. "Don't leave me getting drunk every night with Winston the goldfish. Please."

I stared back at him and returned his smile, even though the thought of sitting back and watching him marry Claudia made my stomach churn.

"This ends in marriage, either way," Ford said. "But wouldn't it be better with you? It's not *real*-real either way. Be my wife, and at least I can promise we'll have fun."

I had to look away. I was speechless. What could I possibly say to his proposal? And could I really live with myself if I spent the rest of my days—the rest of our friendship—sitting across the table from him and Claudia, knowing that I could have stopped it all? No way.

But the thing was...the *real* thing making me hesitate...

Was my brothers.

Both of their marriages had started out as fake. Both of them had entered into a union with formal contracts and the express intention of divorcing after a year, only to discover that they were legitimately in love with their wives and wanted to make their marriage the real thing.

If I agreed to do this with Ford, could I ever truly convince myself that I wasn't secretly hoping it would end up as happily ever after for me as it had for Stefan and Luka? What if I never recovered from the divorce? What if this faux marriage doomed our friendship even more?

I looked back up at him. He was still holding my face, his own expression a mix of hope and good humor. It would be so easy to kiss him if I just lifted onto my toes. I knew he'd kiss me back, too, despite a lack of audience. He'd do it because he'd take it as me agreeing to his plan.

But if I'd learned anything in the past week, it was that fake kisses from Ford felt as good as real ones. If we were married—even if there was a contract, even if we had an understanding—just think how many kisses I could give him over the course of a year.

Maybe enough to make the inevitable heartbreak worth it.

The clock struck two a.m. It was long past midnight. The party was over. I let Ford put me in a private car back to my apartment, dropping my purse, heels, and dress on the hardwood floor as I walked through my living room, the lights of Chicago glowing softly out of the floor-to-ceiling windows. I crawled into bed, pulling a comfortably worn-in old band T-shirt over my head. Then I took a deep breath and stared up at the ceiling, processing what I had done.

Munchkin click-clacked into the room and then leaped up onto the covers next to me, his face tilted curiously as he tried to gauge my mood. He couldn't speak, of course, but he always seemed to know when I was upset or sad. Or confused. He seemed to understand me, sometimes better than the human beings in my life.

"Ford proposed," I told my dog. "In a most unorthodox fashion."

Dropping his chin onto my knee, Munchkin looked up at me, brows knitting together, his big brown eyes full of concern. It was almost like he was asking, "And then what?"

I sat up, pulled him close, and gave him a kiss on the top of his head, right between his pointy little ears.

"Obviously, Munchkin," I whispered into his fur, "I told him yes."

FORD

CHAPTER 11

As soon as I got back to my apartment, my suit was off. After an endless evening like the one I'd just had, buttoned up in my tux, smiling and shaking hands with every last snooty guest, all I wanted was a pair of comfy sweats and total silence. I grabbed a bottle of water from my fridge, downed half of it in one go, and parked my ass on the couch.

Finally. A moment to myself.

Thank God Emzee said yes to my plan.

For a brief moment, I'd seen the refusal on her face, and I was sure she'd back out. It wasn't a small ask, and she'd already done more than enough to help me out with the Claudia situation. But of course she said yes. She always did.

That was one of the reasons we were still such close friends after all these years—she was the kind of person who could roll with the punches, who was always down for whatever crazy schemes I came up with. Dumb stuff like putting on British accents at a college party full of people we didn't know, or committing ourselves to the twenty-five hour and nine minute straight total running time that was the eleven-film Star Wars marathon (she'd even brought over two batches of Storm Trooper cookies), or the year we'd spent Christmas Eve driving all over Chicago to rearrange people's lawn decorations so that pairs of deer appeared to be humping. Emzee had been cool like that ever since high school—ever since I became her "hero."

And tonight, that hero worship shit had really paid off. Because I knew I'd been pushing my luck with this whole charade. In fact, luck was a very good word for what it felt like I had with Emzee in general. How many guys in my position would have ended up with a ride-or-die like her? Still, I'd known that I was skating on thin ice when I dropped the surprise engagement bomb on her with zero warning, right in front of my parents and Claudia. Especially after we'd decided to do the exact opposite and call the whole thing off.

The thing was, once I'd realized how brilliant this plan was, there was no way I could have just walked away. We both knew that my mother never would have stopped until I was shacked up with Claudia and cranking out the grandchildren.

I shuddered at the thought.

Sure, my ex was hot—smoking hot—and yeah, she knew how to walk the walk—but that was about it. She was predictable, she didn't have a sense of humor, and the times she'd flashed her mean streak with Emzee or a valet or a waiter had turned my stomach. The truth was, I'd lost interest in her ages ago. It had just taken me a while to do something about it. The thought of spending my entire life with her made me want to throw myself off the Willis Tower.

The thought of spending my entire life with *anyone*

made me feel that way.

I just wasn't down with the whole ball and chain life-style. I liked my freedom. Liked being able to do whatever I wanted. I was way too young to settle down just yet.

That's why Emzee was the perfect choice for this whole charade. A year married to her would hardly be a hardship at all. She was laid back, fun to hang with, and eager to say yes. In other words: jackpot.

I finished my water, crushed the bottle, and leaned back into the supple, full grain leather of my couch.

I loved my apartment, how completely and utterly masculine it was. Leather and reclaimed wood and steel everything, modern and rustic at the same time. Claudia had always been trying to change it; to change me. First she wanted me to clear out a dresser drawer for her in the bedroom, then she started bugging me to buy new furniture —a velvet Chesterfield, which I vetoed, and a wood frame bed instead of my black platform model, which I agreed to— and then there was the day I came home to find that she'd put a floral shower curtain and matching rugs in the bath-room. That's when I realized she was trying to lock me down, one flowered curtain at a time, and I knew she had to go. I couldn't live like that.

Emzee never would have pulled that kind of shit. She'd never try to change me.

I put my feet up, taking a moment to appreciate how fucking brilliant my plan was. I had to admit, I'd even impressed myself.

Of course, my mother would have preferred Claudia, but I knew she'd come around eventually. After all, a daugh-ter-in-law was a daughter-in-law, and Emzee checked a lot of the same boxes that Claudia did. She'd do the right things and say the right things, and it wasn't like Emzee was some kind of upstart. She was wealthy, and not only that, she'd been a member of Chicago society since she was a child. Like it or not, she was well aware of the ins and outs of the invisible rulebook that governed our social class. She could roll with it.

She even ran her own charity, for fuck's sake, something Claudia had never managed to accomplish. Not that she had ever tried to tackle something like that, but I knew it got under her skin that Emzee had something on her resume that Claudia didn't. My ex had brought it up enough times —completely out of nowhere—that it was obvious the charity's success annoyed her. Claudia couldn't say enough disparaging things about See Yourself. How self-aggrandizing and unnecessary it was, essentially just some vanity project, how it was wasteful to throw all that money away handing out cameras and photography training to a bunch of aged-out models.

I knew Claudia was just jealous, but I'd gotten sick of her trash talk pretty fast. In fact, it had been yet another sturdy nail in the coffin for our relationship. There was nothing wasteful about using one's connections and wealth to help people in need, regardless of who those people were. In fact, helping others was one of the best things a person of privilege—or any person, really—could do in their life. Guess Claudia wasn't familiar with the concept.

No matter, though. She was gone. And this engagement to Emzee meant that Claudia couldn't just manipulate her way back into my life, not even with my mother's help.

I finally had control of my life again.

Everything was coming up Ford.

Letting out a yawn, I checked my phone. It was after three a.m. Time for bed. I padded down the hall and walked into my bedroom, a place that had always been my sanctuary.

It was set up for seduction. A big, luxuriously comfortable king-sized bed dominated the space, covered in expensive, black silk sheets. The lights were dimmable, the curtains dark, the mood beyond sexy. If a woman was in my room, she knew what was about to happen.

Shucking my sweatpants, I slid under the covers naked. It was how I always slept.

How would my blushing bride-to-be react if I carried her over the threshold after our wedding and took her straight here?

As I stretched out on the bed, all my back-patting suddenly gave way to the tiniest hint of guilt. About Emzee. Would she still be my friend at the end of this?

Maybe. Maybe not.

Was I shamelessly exploiting her crush on me to get what I wanted?

Yeah, I was.

She didn't even realize that I knew about her long-held torch for me, but I'd always pretended I was oblivious. I liked our friendship just the way it was, and sex (and the inevitable messy breakup later) would have destroyed us. So I'd always considered to be Emzee off-limits.

Now *that* could be a problem.

Because there was no way I could go a whole year without sex.

Though frankly, I wouldn't mind having it with my new fiancée. It was all I could think about, seeing her in that dress tonight. And it wasn't like it had been any kind of hardship to kiss her all those times—making out with Emzee was hot. I'd even gotten a little turned on when she was pressed right up against me. Who wouldn't? She had those lush tits, that curvy little body, and a pair of the softest, thickest lips I'd ever seen. They'd always looked absolutely prime for giving head; I'd had the thought more than once over our seven years of friendship.

But at the end of the day, she was still a girl. A girl with a crush.

I knew that for her, sex would come with feelings. Lots of them. Under the tough-girl attitude and the dark eye makeup and the boots, Em was secretly a big softie. Her heart was a delicate thing. Shit, I'd witnessed her blinking back actual tears just talking about the sweaters she'd bought for her rescue dog. So yeah, I had to give this sex thing some consideration. Because once we started sleeping together, she'd stop thinking of our relationship as fake.

Which would be a problem when it came time to orchestrate the divorce.

Hell hath no fury like a woman scorned, as they said. It wouldn't do me any good to upset Emzee and give her a reason to seek revenge in court later. She could blow this whole thing up if she wanted to, go to the press with her story, hire a top dollar legal team to get her some massive alimony payment, maybe even try to take my apartment. I'd have to play my cards exactly right throughout all of this. Emzee the best friend would never do anything to hurt me. Emzee the heartbroken ex-wife? I had no idea.

I rubbed my eyes, realizing I'd made a major misstep in not giving more thought to the intimacy aspect of our arrangement. If Emzee and I were married, even if it was for show, I couldn't step out on her, couldn't sleep around. And our chemistry had to be off the charts if we were really going to sell the whole thing. So I'd have to somehow navigate the emotional minefield ahead of me, because abstinence was not an option.

It had been bad enough going without since Claudia and I had broken up—it wasn't intentional celibacy, of course, but I'd been swamped at work for a few weeks, and then I had to focus all my attention on getting my family to believe that Emzee and I were actually together.

At this point, I was starting to get antsy.

My mind wandered back to the dress Emzee had worn tonight. I hadn't been able to stop staring at that open back. How much bare, creamy skin was exposed. I'd had to satisfy myself with running my hand gently up and down her spine all evening, keeping everything G-rated, my fingers itching to slide straight down the fabric and cup her gorgeous ass the whole time.

If our night out had been real, that dress would be in a puddle on my bedroom floor right now. I'd have Emzee lying spreadeagle on the bed, thighs spread wide, making her whimper with pleasure as I gave her a taste of what this cock was capable of.

I felt myself growing hard at the thought.

Sex with her would be good, I had no doubt—we had chemistry, the kiss proved that—but I also knew that Emzee didn't have a lot of experience. Sure, she had dated plenty, but no one had ever lasted long enough to really learn all her hot spots, and I was confident that whomever she'd slept with—mostly self-absorbed artist types in skinny jeans—probably hadn't taken the time or effort to bring her to the explosive orgasms I always provided my sexual partners. I doubted her usual type even knew how. It'd be up to me to chart unknown waters.

I wrapped my hand around my hard cock as I thought about all that would entail. The long, wet kisses, my hands gliding over her curves, her soft moans as her body opened up to me. I would make it good for her. Good for both of us.

And because she was halfway in love with me already, I knew that when the time came to seduce Emzee, she wouldn't say no.

EMZEE

CHAPTER 12

I f I was going to get married, there had to be some structure.

Now that I'd taken the time to really think about what it would mean for me and Ford to walk down the aisle —even if it was just for show—I knew that we needed to lay down some ground rules and guidelines before this went any further.

I'd initially learned a bit about how to set up a sham marriage thanks to watching both of my brothers have theirs arranged—and then later, I'd gotten some of the real nitty-gritty, behind-the-scenes stuff via conversations with The Wives. I had a pretty good idea of what needed to happen before anyone said "I do." In fact, at this point, I felt like a bit of an expert on the subject.

Now I had to get Ford on the same page.

I'd texted him that morning, telling him to meet me at my place because, and I quote, "Munchkin has spent way too much time without me lately, and I think he misses you too." I knew it would get him to agree; Ford loved my little guy, and the feeling was mutual.

In reality, it was just an excuse to stay on my turf for now. There was no way I'd be comfortable meeting up at the country club again, or at that shag pad of a bachelor apartment Ford lived in. Especially when this conversation was going to be so loaded.

While I waited for him to arrive, I tidied things up.

My gorgeous timber loft in River North was more like a big studio than a proper apartment, with twelve-foot ceilings, exposed beams, and these amazing, massive windows that made the place ideal for independent photo shoots. Instead of separate rooms with walls, the loft was split into areas—a kitchen area, a living room area, an office nook where I edited photos.

It had been love at first sight—I still remember the first time I stepped foot across the threshold, after a long, fruitless day of apartment tours with a real estate agent. The second we walked in, I gasped, grabbed her arm, and told her I'd take it. What had sold me on the spot was the huge open floor plan, the all-original, banged-up, hundred-year-old wood floors, and the cute little bedroom tucked off to the side of the long entry hallway. And that was before I'd even seen the master bathroom with its big soaking tub that was tucked away in the corner of the space.

Ford appreciated the loft, too. It's where we'd always hung out, since his apartment was such an obvious bachelor pad. At least, until Claudia started "decorating." Between the flowery rugs she'd put in the bathroom, the ruffly curtains she'd hung up in the kitchen, and the piles of overembellished, girly throw pillows she'd added to the sofa, the place had gotten a lot more Claudia than Ford over the years, and no way did I enjoy being over there. Luckily, it had never caused an issue. Ford was more than happy to kick back at my place.

Speaking of which, even though I knew we'd be talking in the living room or the open kitchen area, I still cleaned my bedroom from top to bottom. Still made the bed, fluffed the pillows, adjusted the blanket tossed over the end. Just in case he glanced in as he walked by. I didn't want him thinking his potential new wife was a total slob.

My doorbell rang, and Munchkin took off to investigate. He must have known it was Ford, because instead of yipping and yapping, he sat down in front of the door and anxiously waited for me to open it. Which I did right away, only to find my favorite version of my best friend standing there. This was the casual, Saturday afternoon Ford, in a pair of jeans, a tight gray T-shirt, and with his hair adorably tousled as if he'd just rolled out of bed.

"Well. If it isn't my beautiful wife-to-be and my furry little future stepson," he said, crouching down to pat Munchkin before sweeping me into a hug.

I savored the feel of his arms tight around me for a moment, then forced myself to focus and step back.

"None of that from you," I chided him. "We're here to talk business."

"Ooh," he said, giving me a wink. "I love it when you're all stern and tough."

Ignoring the teasing, I gestured for him to take a seat on the sectional in the living room area. I'd made a fairly comprehensive list of the things we needed to go over, and Ford raised his eyebrows when he saw it on the coffee table.

"Wow," he said. "This looks serious."

I gave him a look. "You said we'd have a contract," I reminded him. "So I figured we'd better get together and hammer out the details to this lie."

"You're the boss," he said. Then he looked down at my dog, who was sitting on the floor gazing at Ford with eyes of love, his stump of a tail wiggling. "Come here, bud, it's been a while," Ford said, hoisting Munchkin onto his lap and scratching him behind the ears.

It was hard not to melt at the sight of my two favorite dudes enjoying each other's company. "You want a drink or something? I have your Pappy whatever in the cupboard."

"Little early for bourbon," he said, "but I appreciate that."

"Okay," I said, trying to sound detached and professional. "Let's get down to business."

"Yes, ma'am," Ford said, even giving me a cheeky salute.

I bit back a smile and read the first item on my list. "First off, what is the length of our arrangement?"

"A year? Year and a half?" Ford bit his lip as he considered, and I stared at his mouth, remembering how it had felt to kiss him. If I agreed to this, I'd be kissing him a lot more. I had no idea how I was going to protect my heart from getting broken once this whole thing was over.

I cleared my throat. "Let's split the difference and say fifteen months. I actually thought we were only planning for a year."

"We are," Ford said. "One year of marriage and three months of engagement."

"Ah. Right." I wrote that down.

"It's perfect," he added. "After a quickie engagement, people won't be as surprised when we get divorced a year later. In fact, we can use that as part of the excuse."

"Because we rushed into things," I said.

"Exactly!"

He didn't seem to notice that I didn't have any of the same excitement in my voice as he did in his.

"Living arrangements?" I said, moving on to the next item on my list.

Ford was scratching behind Munchkin's ears. "We'll live at my place, of course," he said.

"Ha!" I blurted out. "Are you joking? No way am I giving up my loft."

"Come on, Em," he scoffed. "This place has no walls."

I frowned. "The bedroom has walls. So does the bathroom."

"But my place has a separate office for my work from home days. Where am I supposed to go when you have models here for shoots? I can't just lock myself in your bedroom all day, the room's the size of a closet. *My* apartment has lots of actual rooms. Big ones. With walls *and* doors. Doors that can be closed. Besides, your place gets downright frigid in the winter."

"That's what the space heater is for," I pointed out. "This is nonnegotiable."

Ford let out a sigh, perplexed enough that he'd stopped petting my dog. "We can't have separate apartments. We need people to believe this marriage is real."

"I know," I said.

"And the fact is, my apartment works better," he said. "It's nicer, a hell of a lot newer, it has more square footage, and last but not least, I have multiple bedrooms."

I frowned. We'd have to get to that part of the contract eventually.

"I get what you're saying, but I don't want to lose my place," I said. "This whole thing is temporary, so I can't just dismantle my entire life and then try to rebuild it when we're done."

Ford let out a long breath. "That's fair. So what are you suggesting? You want to sublet it to a friend? Airbnb the place?"

Shaking my head, I said, "None of the above. Why don't

I just keep paying rent here while I'm staying with you and we can call it my official studio? You have your office at home, I have mine here. Nobody's going to question it."

"Fine," he said. "I have no problem with that."

I nodded, and made a note on my list. *Live at Ford's, MZ keeps her place for work.*

"And Munchkin comes with me," I said. "Obviously."

"Obviously," Ford said with a grin.

I smiled down at my dog, who was now snoring away in Ford's lap.

"He's not a shedder, is he?" Ford asked, but I could tell that he was joking.

"Next item," I said. "Who knows the truth about our marriage being a contract?"

"No one," Ford said. "We can't risk it getting out that this is fake."

Crossing my arms, I argued, "I mean, I at least need to tell my brothers."

Ford shook his head. "No way."

"Seriously? You know I hate lying," I said. "Especially between family members. My brothers and I have already been through so much with our dad, and I'm sick of it. I don't want to perpetuate a legacy of, like, secrets and obfuscation and bullshit. Don't you get that?"

I was getting very worked up, and Ford held up his hands. "Look, Em, I do get it. But the less people who know, the better. I don't trust anyone to keep their mouths shut—"

"How do you not trust Stefan and Luka?" I countered. "They've both done the whole fake marriage thing before —if anything, they know how important it is to keep a secret like this. They'd be super supportive and understanding."

Ford gave me a look. "There is no version of reality

where I see your brothers being supportive of me fake-marrying their little sister," he said.

I supposed he did have a point. Stefan and Luka were extremely protective of me.

"They'd be able to give us advice," I tried again.

"Oh, I bet they would. That's the whole problem. Because of your brothers' experiences, they're going to think this whole thing will eventually become real, the way it did for them," he said. "So why not let them think that's the case all along? Less stories to keep straight."

Dammit. "You have a point," I conceded.

"Go on," Ford said, gesturing toward my pad. "Write it down."

We tell no one the truth, was what I wrote.

Except The Wives, I thought to myself. I knew I could trust them, though. And it didn't seem like a good idea to mention that I'd already told my sisters-in-law about Ford's original fake-dating proposal. If we got married, they'd likely assume it was an extension of that sham.

Ford and I spent the next thirty minutes hammering out the rest of our agreement, the story we were going to tell people, the way we were going to live our lives, both of us committing to public events to prove that we were the real deal. I'd go to Malone Real Estate Holdings events over the next few months, while Ford would attend fundraisers for my charity.

I was staring down at the remainder of my list, at all the notes I'd made, when Ford cleared his throat.

"As for us...if we're going to make this seem real, we can't be getting any side action."

Ah. So he'd decided to bring up the awkward part. "No, definitely not," I agreed.

"We should probably discuss how we can make this the most comfortable for both of us."

"O...kay?" I said, not following. Did we really need to talk about celibacy?

Ford lifted Munchkin off his lap and placed him on the floor. He padded over to his favorite bed next to the couch, plopping down and going back to sleep.

Reaching over, Ford put his hand on mine. Tiny, hot sparks spread up my arm.

"Em, we're going to have to really sell this," he clarified, eyes locking on mine.

Oh. It had taken me a second to figure out what he was actually hinting at. My mouth went dry. Meanwhile my face, my chest, my entire body, everything felt like it was on fire.

"We can't hook up, Ford," I said. "It would ruin our friendship."

If the whole fake marriage thing didn't do that first.

Ford leaned back, still regarding me with that intense, searching stare. "Will it, though? Are you not attracted to me?"

"I don't like this conversation," I said, knowing my blush was probably giving me away.

"Because I'm definitely attracted to you," he went on.

All the air seemed to leave my body at once. It was the *worst* thing he could have said.

"You are?" I managed to sputter.

My heart was already entering into this contract with foolish hope. Between my brothers' experiences with their arranged-marriages-turned-real and my unrequited school-girl crush on Ford, I was already wondering if things between us might actually shift from fake to real.

Which I knew was only setting me up for inevitable disappointment and heartache.

Which was why we most *definitely* could not hook up.

I had to stay true to that conviction. I was undoubtedly going to lose my heart over the course of this arrangement. I didn't want to lose my virginity, too. The less I lost, the better.

"It's not a good idea," I said. "We need to keep things uncomplicated."

"I disagree," Ford said with a wicked smile. "I think it's a very, very good idea."

It was hard to not just give in right away—right here and now—when he was looking at me that way. After all, hadn't I waited seven years for Ford to say he was attracted to me?

But I needed to stay strong.

"It's a no," I said firmly.

Ford leaned back, still grinning, obviously not taking no for an answer.

"How about we put a pin in it, until we see how things are going," he said. "We don't have to decide everything right now."

"Yeah, I guess we don't," I agreed—though I knew that this was the one thing we definitely *should* have decided beforehand. Still, I didn't have the energy (or the will) to argue about it at the moment. Especially since the next thing on our list was going to take a lot of it.

"News about our engagement is already spreading," I told Ford. "Which means I have to tell my brothers. Tonight."

He nodded. "I figured. Should I come with you?"

I shook my head. "I can do it myself," I told him. "It'll be safer this way."

Just in case one of them got punch-y.

EMZEE

CHAPTER 13

Before my father had gone to prison, our rare Zoric family dinners had always been tense and awkward. My father liked maintaining the illusion of a big, happy, united family, but when it came down to it, our actual happiness mattered zilch to him. All he ever cared about was power and money and optics, and us kids were only useful to him as one more means to that end. We weren't emotionally close to him, but he liked to keep us physically close. He had expectations that we'd show up for various events and meetings to make him look good. I'd hated it.

Now that he was out of the picture and both of my brothers were in solid marriages with babies on the way, our family dinners were more frequent and less horribly uncomfortable.

That had a lot to do with Tori, who loved hosting us at the gorgeous luxury condo she and Stefan lived in. The apartment itself had even become more welcoming since their marriage had solidified. Before, it had been all dark masculine furniture and starkly modern, almost bare rooms.

But Tori had put up family photos, switched out the heavy curtains for airy linen ones, even painted some of the walls in soothing shades of blue. Now, it felt more like a home.

I could really appreciate it.

I didn't know all the details about Tori's life before Stefan, but I'd gathered that her senator father (may he rest in peace) had been a lot like ours; concerned more with appearances than the actual well-being of his children. Tori had a stepmother named Michelle, though—a true southern belle who was loving and kind and had tried to make their house a home—and Tori seemed determined to do the same for us Zoric siblings. My sister-in-law was going to be an amazing mom. We certainly all benefited from having her around.

I used my key to let myself in, and immediately heard voices coming from the kitchen.

"The party has arrived!" I announced, heading toward the noise.

Tori and Brooklyn greeted me warmly. I got a hug and a kiss from both of them, though Tori's huge, pregnant belly got a bit in the way of the hug.

"You look amazing," I told her with a grin. "Are you getting excited about the delivery?"

She laughed. "I just want this baby out of me. I'm more than ready for it."

"And I'm ready to hear all your advice," Brooklyn chimed in. "I know I'm barely showing, but I feel like I've been knocked up for a million years."

"Your morning sickness still acting up?" I asked.

Brooklyn gave a shudder. "It's the fucking worst, I swear. I miss being able to keep down my breakfast. Speaking of food..."

Apparently they'd been deep in discussion about the

scalloped potato recipe being served for dinner. I could smell the dreamy, cheesy, buttery goodness cooking in the oven.

"I just don't get why mine always turn rock hard," Brooklyn said. "Or else the milk curdles. I've basically given up at this point, even though I love them."

"Three things," Tori said, holding up her fingers. "One: Yukon Gold potatoes only. You can't be using red skinned or anything like that."

"The recipe specifically said red skin!" Brooklyn said. "It's a conspiracy!"

Grinning, Tori said, "Trust me. Yukon only. Two: you have to slice with a mandoline. No knife is ever going to cut them thin enough, that's a fact. And three: you must use whole milk, or even fifty-fifty milk and cream. These are the great secrets, directly from Michelle."

"I'm ready to follow your ways, Tori-wan," Brooklyn joked, crouching down to peek at the dish bubbling away in the oven. "They look amazing."

"Actually, if potatoes is the only thing baby wants you to eat, I've got another Michelle recipe tucked into one of my books around here somewhere," Tori said, turning to rummage through a stack of cookbooks on a shelf.

Through the kitchen doorway, I saw my brothers in the living room, congregating by the bar. Stefan caught my eye and jerked his chin, indicating that I should join them for a mini-meeting while The Wives were distracted. I politely excused myself from the potato discussion and headed toward Stefan. He was pouring out glasses of scotch, muttering as he did so. He and Luka both looked tense. My stomach dropped. This couldn't be good.

Stefan slid a drink over to me, and we all took a somber sip before anyone spoke.

"The Bratva would like their money," Stefan said. "And soon."

Adrenaline rushed through me, and I took another long swallow of the scotch.

"We don't have it," Luka hissed. "In case you hadn't noticed, we aren't a very liquid company right now."

"I'm aware," Stefan said sharply, his voice hushed. "And I'm doing everything I can to stall. I even told them how we've been rebuilding, and that we just narrowly avoided a takeover by Elite. But they don't give a shit about our excuses. Crime *was* paying, after all."

Stefan tossed the rest of his drink back and poured himself another.

"Jesus fuck. We could actually lose everything," I murmured.

"That's real helpful, Em," Luka said. "How big of a loan can we take out as a business?"

"Not an option." Stefan shook his head. "Even if we could borrow that much, or even half, we'd be fucked at tax time. You have to be able to itemize and account for that kind of—"

"And just what are we all whispering about?" Brooklyn asked brightly, appearing out of nowhere.

We all jumped, doing our best to act natural—and probably failing.

"I, um, was just telling my brothers that I have a surprise," I said. Three pairs of eyes turned to me, and I scrambled for something to say. "I'm, uh...well, I'm engaged!"

It wasn't exactly how I'd planned to spring the news on everyone tonight, but my brothers and I had needed to come up with a distraction and this was a pretty handy one.

For a moment, everyone just stared. Then their eyes darted down to my hand.

"I don't have a ring yet!" I said quickly, putting my hands behind my back. "We're trying to get his grandmother's. It has sentimental value."

"You're engaged," Stefan said, his voice flat, as if he didn't quite believe me.

"Yep!" I said, keeping my own voice cheery.

"Oh my God!" Brooklyn said, throwing her arms around me and jumping up and down. "Congratulations, Emzee! Emzee's getting married!"

"Emzee's getting married?" Tori echoed, rushing into the room as fast as her pregnant body could take her. She joined Brooklyn so us girls were all in a group hug now.

"To who?" Luka asked skeptically. "I didn't know you were even dating anybody."

My brothers seemed pretty taken aback. Not least because they probably couldn't figure out if I'd just come up with the story on the spot to cover for our sibling huddle. There'd be no reason for them to be suspicious, though, once they heard who it was.

"To Ford," I said, trying to keep my tone light.

"Really?" Stefan said, not disguising his shock.

My brothers knew who Ford was—and what he was to me. They knew he'd protected me from the high school bullies who'd made my life hell and that the two of us had been close ever since. He'd been a fixture in my life for years. A very platonic fixture, however.

"Wait, you're marrying *Ford*?" Brooklyn said.

"Hmm," Tori said, narrowing her eyes at me a little, sizing me up.

I couldn't blame The Wives for being taken aback as well—considering the fact that the last they heard, Ford was supposed to be my fake (and temporary) boyfriend. They were clearly bursting to drill me for all the details about the unexpected escalation, but luckily they were bound by the Secrets of the Vault not to disclose what they already knew in front of my brothers.

Still, I knew I'd be getting the third degree during our next lunch.

"Yes, I am," I answered Brooklyn. "We haven't picked a date yet, but probably in the next few months. I know it seems sudden, but...I guess when you know, you know."

There was another long silence—The Wives exchanging glances and my brothers doing the same. I held my breath.

And then a smile spread across Stefan's face.

"This is great news," he said. "Malone's exactly the right kind of man for this family."

I let out a relieved laugh. Out of everyone, I valued Stefan's approval the most. After all, since our father had gone to prison, my oldest brother had taken over as head of the household.

"This calls for a celebration," Luka announced.

"There's champagne in the fridge!" Tori said, heading into the kitchen.

Stefan popped the bubbly open and poured a glass for everyone, including a few sips' worth for both of the pregnant Wives.

"I'd like to raise a toast to the joyful union of Emzee and our future brother-in-law, Ford," Stefan said as we all lifted our glasses. "We'll have to invite him over for the next dinner and properly welcome him into the family."

Everyone started talking all at once about how happy and supportive they were, how beneficial it would be for someone in the Zoric family to make a match with a son of the Malones. I washed down my guilt with all the champagne that The Wives couldn't drink. There was nothing I could do but just go with it. The family deserved some good news, after all.

Across the top of my champagne flute, I caught Tori's gaze. She lifted her eyebrows in a questioning manner and I shot her a pleading look. This wasn't the time to talk about it.

"It actually makes perfect sense," Luka said. "You two have known each other forever."

"Yep," I said, drinking more champagne. "Shall we sit down and eat?"

Once dinner was over, I insisted that my brothers leave us women alone to have some girl talk while we loaded up the dishwasher and tidied up the kitchen.

"What happened?" Tori wanted to know, a sly grin spreading across her face.

"I thought this was a temporary thing," Brooklyn teased. "Did you take my advice to bang him and he ended up proposing on the spot?"

"Of course not!" My cheeks went hot. "Look, I can't talk about it just yet, but please do not breathe *a word* to my brothers about the origin story," I said, lowering my voice. "I promise I'll fill you in later. For now...just roll with it," I said.

Oh, the irony.

EMZEE

CHAPTER 14

Now that our families had been told about the engagement, it was time to break the news to our friends. Or rather, Ford's friends.

It wasn't until we had sat down and discussed all the people we needed to tell that I realized how few people I actually hung out with other than Ford—after all, I hadn't been popular in high school, my art school co-eds from college were more like casual acquaintances, and I traveled so much for work that the only friendships I really maintained were with Tori and Brooklyn, who already knew what was up with my whirlwind relationship.

Thus, the group we were planning to meet up with definitely consisted of more of his circle than mine. Unfortunately, they were mostly people we'd gone to high school with...not my main tormentors, but they'd certainly gone along with the torture I endured. And all these years later, they were still very cliquey. No matter how many times Ford had brought me along to socialize with them, I still didn't quite feel tight with the group. I'd never have even been a blip on their radar if it hadn't been for Ford taking me under his wing.

Did I want to spend a whole night out with them? Hells no.

But these were Ford's closest cohorts, and he wanted us to share our news together.

He had a whole big event planned to celebrate, with all of us going out to his favorite club, drinking and dancing until the sun came up.

I was anxious about the whole thing, which was how I always felt when I hung out with this particular group. It would have been easier for me to just stay home and let Ford tell them the news on his own, but I knew he wanted them to see us together.

"We really need to sell it," he'd said. "It has to look 100% real."

It was already far too real for me. How was I going to survive the next fifteen months?

"Oh, and don't forget to wear something hot," he'd reminded me earlier that evening.

Right. I couldn't help remembering the way he had looked at me the night of the ball—how his eyes kept straying to my exposed back, how his warm hands had trailed up and down my spine, lingering right over my ass. The thought of dressing up for him again made my skin tingle. Especially knowing that we were going to be performing tonight.

Though I was kind of glad to have the show of lovebird-ness to make me feel more included. It gave me a thrill of anticipation, outweighing the usual dread I felt when I knew I'd be hanging out with his friends. After all this time, I'd long forgiven them, but I'd never forget how cruel they were in high school.

Maybe tonight would be different, though. Maybe I'd finally be welcomed into the group.

After doing my hair and makeup—sleek ponytail and smoky eyes with a dark lip—I laid out a few outfit options on my bed and tried to decide exactly how hot I wanted to look for Ford.

The answer, in the end, was very, very hot.

I scarcely recognized myself as I caught a glimpse in the mirror on my way out. The dress I'd pulled from the back of my closet was way shorter than anything I'd normally wear, and the shimmery silver fabric hugged every curve, leaving almost nothing to the imagination.

It was hard not to feel even more exposed given that the color was outside the realm of my usual basic black, but I liked the way the silver made my hair look even darker and my skin even paler, giving me a very dramatic, attention-getting look that was unusual for me.

I liked the way the dress showed off my short but shapely legs, clinging to my thighs. I liked the way it was snug around my hips and waist, while the cowl neckline dipped down, showing off just a hint of cleavage.

I hoped this was what Ford had been asking for. I had really gone all out.

Even my go-to lace up shitkickers had been ditched in favor of knee-high boots with a dangerous heel, and I'd added a pair of diamond stud earrings and a small clutch that slipped over my wrist as the finishing touches.

Ford met me in the lobby of my building.

He was facing away when the elevator doors opened, so I had the opportunity to stare a little. He looked good, as usual, in a tailored black shirt and well-fitting jeans. I wondered if he had dressed in black in an effort to match me, and if he'd be disappointed that I wasn't in my usual uniform.

But when he turned and saw me, the look in his eyes made it very, very clear that he wasn't disappointed at all.

"Fuck," he said, before letting out a low whistle. "You look sexy as hell, Em."

I flushed at the reaction. "Thanks," I said. "You look nice, too."

"Oh, I know," he said and gave me a wink. "Shall we?"

He held out his arm and I wrapped my hand around his rock-hard bicep, trying to remember why I had been so hesitant to come out tonight. If the rest of the evening was like this, maybe I'd have fun after all.

Tension vibrated between the two of us as we were driven to the club. At one point, Ford reached over and took my hand, his fingers sliding over my knuckles.

"Sorry I haven't taken care of the ring yet," he said. "I'm working on it."

"It's okay," I said, even though I knew it would probably come up tonight.

After all, even my brothers had noticed I wasn't wearing one, and they weren't exactly the type to pay attention to something like that. Ford's friends would definitely notice.

"I really want to get you my great-grandmother's ring," he said, sounding determined.

I looked at him. He'd mentioned that at the ball, to his mother, but I'd thought he was just ribbing her, knowing it would bother her. I didn't actually think he was serious. I also didn't think his mother would willingly give that ring to someone like me. In any case, I wasn't holding my breath. Even if it *was* extra beautiful and had its own cool little history.

"We don't need to use that ring. We can just get whatever. From a jewelry store with a good return policy, maybe?" I tried to joke lightly.

"No," Ford said, lifting my knuckles to his mouth in a surprisingly tender gesture. "I want you to have hers."

It wasn't until we arrived at the club that my nerves kicked back into high gear.

I spotted Ford's friends sitting in the VIP area that Ford had reserved ahead of time. There were already buckets of champagne chilling on the table and a tray of shots lined up waiting for us. As we headed over, we were greeted by a round of raucous cheering that made it clear everyone had already started drinking. If Ford's friends were surprised to see me, they hid it well. And no one commented on the fact that Ford and I were holding hands.

Instead, I was welcomed with warm greetings from the guys and air kisses from the girls.

"So what'd you pull us all together for?" one of the guys asked once we'd settled in.

"I have an announcement to make," Ford said, making sure everyone had a filled champagne glass. "Emzee and I— we're getting married!"

I expected silence or shock, but no one was more shocked than me when the immediate response was loud cheering, raised glasses, and nothing but smiling, excited faces all around.

"To Ford and Emzee!" they toasted.

We clinked glasses and drank, and I leaned back against the plush velvet of the VIP seat, trying to roll with the fact that my status had instantly changed the second I'd walked in on Ford's arm, and that it would probably stay that way now that everyone knew I was his fiancée. Even without a ring on my finger, Ford's friends just accepted us as a couple right on the spot.

Everyone was friendly and charming to me, complimenting me on my dress and my boots and my purse. I took it all in with a gracious smile.

"This definitely isn't a surprise to me," one of Ford's guy friends said after we'd all gone through a bottle of champagne. "You two have been friends for ages."

"Totally," one of the girls said. "It makes perfect sense. A lot more sense than Claud—" But she was cut off from speaking the name of She Who Must Not Be Named by her friend.

"I knew you guys were banging," another girl said, her voice a sotto whisper close to my ear. "I mean, how could you and Ford be friends for so long and not be?"

The girl who'd been elbowed into silence a second ago laughed. "Too true."

"We weren't—" I started to correct, and then remembered myself. Better to lean into the speculation. After all, if people wanted to think that Ford and I had been carrying on some secret affair, it could only lend more credibility to our quickie engagement and marriage.

I cleared my throat.

"We weren't telling anyone," I said, leaning my head on Ford's shoulder in a way that I hoped seemed couple-y. "What can I say? We're good at keeping things hush-hush."

"At least I am," Ford interjected with a wicked leer. "Em's actually a bit of a screamer."

Everyone laughed and Ford accepted high fives.

I felt my face go hot, and I couldn't help feeling equally thrilled and uncomfortable at Ford's casual discussion of our fictional sex life.

Okay, maybe more thrilled than uncomfortable. Especially when I imagined what sort of things Ford would do to make me scream.

Like pulling me into the alley behind the club and pressing me up against the wall, his hands sliding up the back of my short dress until he discovered that I was wearing a thong.

Or sneaking me into one of the unisex bathrooms with him, bending me over the sink, my dress hiked up to my waist, his jeans around his knees as he thrust into me from behind, his fingers twisting my nipples hard and perfect.

No, I couldn't think about that. Though it was hard not to when we were constantly touching. And God, was his touch provocative. Especially as the night wore on, and the group began to migrate from our little VIP corner onto the dance floor.

I'd never noticed how tactile Ford was until tonight. Or no, I guess I had. I'd certainly noticed how often he touched his previous girlfriends, like Claudia. It had been hard not to get jealous over the way they'd always been all over each other. How different—and amazing—it was to suddenly be on the other side of that. And also, how confusing.

Ever since we'd left my apartment, Ford's hands had barely left my body. He either had his fingers linked with mine or he was looping an arm around my waist or dragging a finger across the sensitive skin of my collarbone or my earlobe or my bare shoulder. He also liked to tug the ends of my hair, sending sparks of electricity dancing across my scalp. God.

It was even more intense when we danced. He loved to pull me close, his hips moving provocatively against mine, his palms hot against the thin fabric of my dress, cupping all my curves. He kept touching my ass too, his fingers sliding boldly over the crease between my cheeks, as if he was memorizing my body. Every last inch of it.

My pulse was hammering, my skin buzzing at every

point of contact, and the place between my legs was aching and undeniably wet. The air in the club felt hot and thick, and even though I'd only had a glass of champagne and a single shot, I felt drunk. Drunk on desire. Drunk on lust. Drunk on Ford.

There was only so much I could take.

Midway through the night, after dancing chest-to-chest and thigh-to-thigh with Ford had me riled up enough that I knew I needed to step away, I excused myself and went to the bathroom. Once I was there, I pressed a wet paper towel to the back of my neck and between my breasts, trying to cool down and calm the sexual thoughts wreaking havoc on all of my senses. Then I freshened up my makeup and strutted back toward our table.

I was just in time to catch the tail end of a conversation Ford was having with one of his best buddies. Someone he'd been especially close with in high school. The music was loud so I only caught a few words, but what I thought I heard was him asking Ford, "Does Emzee know about that?"

It was enough to stop me in my tracks at the edge of the VIP area. The words were said so conspiratorially that I almost didn't want to ask, but obviously I needed to know the truth.

"Know about what?" I asked loudly.

Ford's friend immediately looked up at me, but before he could answer, Ford flashed him a look I didn't catch and then grinned at me, answering, "About how big my dick is."

Everyone laughed, reverting back to poking fun at me and Ford, and the moment to delve deeper was lost. I laughed too, even though I was sure they'd been talking about something else. The look Ford had given his friend was definitely suspicious, but the group had once again moved on to dirty talk, which I couldn't help focusing on.

Not just the way it made me feel—which, yeah, it made me go hot and tingly in all the right places—but also about Ford's motives with all of this.

Was this how he always joked around about the women he was dating? Or was he laying it on thick because he was trying to push the lie?

Or...what if he was expecting something from me that I couldn't give?

I'd been firm with him about us not sleeping together, but I didn't have enough experience with actual sex to know what would happen afterward. Would it really hurt our relationship if we ended up getting together like that? I was starting to think I should at least consider the possibility.

Especially if Ford was as good in bed as he thought he was.

EMZEE

CHAPTER 15

At two in the morning, we finally left the club. Ford and I slid into the back seat of the car he'd called to take us home, the plan being that I'd get dropped off first and then the driver would take Ford to his place.

I knew all our friends would assume we'd be going home together—that was the whole point of leaving in the same car, of course—which would keep up appearances and ensure this whole charade continued looking legit.

Friends.

I supposed I'd be seeing a lot more of them now. No doubt we'd all be getting together on the regular. Going out. Getting drunk. Having fun. It hadn't exactly been fun for me personally, though I had enjoyed dancing with Ford... but then again, it hadn't been as bad as I'd thought it would be. Hopefully it would all start to feel more natural as time went on. Maybe I'd actually feel like I was part of the group, instead of the awkward outsider that Ford was forcing his friends to be nice to.

Truthfully, it had taken me a while to warm up to Tori

and Brooklyn, too. I'd never been the kind of person who opened up easily. Yet another residual scar from all the bullying I experienced at school.

I leaned back against the seat as Ford gave the driver our addresses. I was tired and more than a little drunk and after all that dancing, my feet were killing me. My boots were great to look at, but they were murder on my toes. I couldn't wait to get home and take them off.

But I also knew that Ford and I had some unfinished business.

Ever since I'd overheard the tail end of that conversation Ford had been having with his friend at the VIP table earlier, I hadn't been able to shake the feeling that something was going on behind my back. So the second the driver rolled up the tinted glass partition, creating a quiet little cocoon in the back seat, I turned to Ford to confront him.

He was slouching, leaned back against the headrest, eyes closed. Obviously tired, and probably more than a little tipsy still—but maybe those things would help me get my answers.

"What was that thing you guys were talking about earlier?" I asked him.

"Hmm?" His eyes were still closed.

Part of me thought about just letting it go, letting the evening go down as a success without poking Ford to answer a question that maybe I didn't even really want answered.

But I also knew that if we were going to do this (and it didn't really seem like we had any other choice, now that everyone in our lives thought we were getting married), I needed Ford to know he couldn't just hide stuff from me and get away with it.

"The conversation I overheard when I got back from the bathroom," I said. "When your friend was like, 'Does Emzee know?' What was that all about?"

"My dick," he said, looking at me now. "I told you that."

There was a smile playing on the corner of his lips and it was impossible not to be a little charmed by the whole thing, but still, I pushed.

"That wasn't it," I said, though I was pretty sure it did have something to do with sex.

My suspicion was only reinforced when he grabbed my hand and gave me a wicked grin.

"You know I have to save a few secrets for the honeymoon, Em," he said.

I rolled my eyes, but my heart was hammering in my chest at the thought of it. "We're not a real couple, remember?" I reminded him. "The honeymoon is just for show."

"That's not what our friends think," Ford said.

"Fair enough. But while we're on the topic..." I shifted to face him, my knee up on the seat between us, the hem of my dress inching higher.

I saw Ford's eyes dart to where all that skin was showing, and felt a little thrill at the heat I saw in his gaze. I cleared my throat and he looked back up at me.

"Why the hell do you keep making all those sex jokes?"

Ford shifted, a more serious expression crossing his face. "I think the real question is, why does me talking about sex make you so uncomfortable?" he said. "It's an honest question."

He put his hand on my knee, the heat from his palm, spreading through me like a fire.

"I don't know," I said, looking away.

"I think I know why. In fact, I'd bet money on it," Ford

said, his thumb drawing a slow, sexy circle on the inside of my knee.

I swallowed hard, waiting for him to go on.

"I think you secretly like it," Ford said, his voice dropping into a low, seductive whisper.

My throat was dry as Ford's hand moved upward, just an inch, but I felt his touch like a shock through my system.

"And that you're uncomfortable because you like it—the sex jokes, thinking about sex, imagining having sex...with me—and you're ashamed of that," he said. "But you shouldn't be."

His voice was like velvet over my senses, his hand stroking the inside of my thigh.

Fuck him for hitting the nail on the head so perfectly. All of Ford's sex jokes, all of his dirty comments, the innuendo, all of it had led to me thinking almost nonstop about having sex with him this entire night out. How it would feel, how good it could be with him—with someone who knew me so well, who had as much experience as he did.

And I did feel ashamed. Even more so because he knew exactly what was going on with me. It was hard not to be humiliated by my interest, my obvious horniness.

Not that I was going to admit it to him. Because Ford didn't need to know he was right. He didn't need the satisfaction. His ego was already big enough.

His dick too, apparently.

I shook those thoughts from my head.

"You're wrong," I said, but my throat was so dry that my denial came out breathy.

Completely undermining the point I was trying to make.

"Am I?" Ford asked. "So if I keep going right now, if I

keep sliding my hand up your skirt, I won't find anything, will I? Because I think I'd like to test my little theory."

I gulped. "I don't know what you're talking about."

I could have pressed my knees together. I could have stopped him. But I didn't.

"Oh no?" Ford gave me that wicked grin again. "So you're telling me that if I put my hand under this slutty little skirt of yours, I won't find a soaking wet pussy waiting for me?"

I was speechless. Ford had never spoken to me this way.

And I fucking loved it. I was eating it up. His words were beyond hot, and so was the hand moving slowly and surely up my inner thigh, mere inches from my hot core.

I could have easily pushed him away. Could have put my purse on my lap. Could have crossed my legs.

Instead, I let them fall open. I gave him full access.

"Mmm, that's nice," Ford said, his hand moving up. "I think I'm about to find out that I am absolutely. Fucking. Right."

I shook my head, even though I knew how wet I was. For him. I could feel it.

"No?" Ford asked.

I could tell that he liked teasing me. And as turned on as I was, it was also infuriating that he could read me so easily. I decided not to make things too easy for him. The parted legs were about as much encouragement as he was going to get.

Not that he seemed to mind.

His hand kept sliding higher, his fingers hot and sure of their destination. I took a deep breath as he neared the apex of my thighs. This wasn't the first time someone had fingered me, but it had only happened once before, and it hadn't been all that good. In fact, it was awful.

The guy's fingers had been too rough, too fast, and when it started to hurt I'd blurted out some random excuse about how I had work early in the morning and then bolted from the guy's apartment, never to return again. Not that I'd ever admit my inexperience to Ford.

This was different, though. I could already tell. Ford had barely even touched me yet, and already I could feel my thighs trembling. I wanted him to do more to me.

"Oh, now what is this?" he asked.

His fingers brushed against the damp lace of my thong, and I nearly bucked off of the seat with the potent pleasure of it.

He grinned. "I knew it," he said, his finger stroking me through the lace again. Up and down, tracing my pussy lips through the fabric, applying just enough pressure to make me shiver.

"Is that a thong under there?" Ford asked, running his finger along the length of it. "Naughty, naughty girl."

I sucked in a breath as he pulled it aside, his fingers touching my opening.

"So wet," he murmured, his eyes locking on mine. "You are so fucking wet for me."

All I could do was let out a little gasp, letting my head fall back as his finger parted me, teasing my slick entrance. I gripped the seat for dear life, worried I'd punch holes in the leather with my nails as Ford slid his finger inside me. Smooth, strong, and sure. Pushing deeper into my wetness, feeling so good I could barely stand it.

"This pussy wants me," he said, moving his finger in and out, pumping softly.

I shook my head no and he laughed.

"You can lie to me, but your pussy can't," he said. "You want this."

He slipped another finger inside, stretching me a little bit, starting to move faster. I liked it. No, I fucking loved it. His fingers felt incredible as they fucked me. In and out, getting faster but not too fast, curling just enough to rub my walls, sensations sparking through me, the hot friction building with every thrust.

My legs were wide open now, my body humming with pleasure, and yet I wanted more. I wanted his mouth on mine, covering my nipples, sucking, biting, trailing kisses up to my neck.

I wanted him, all of him, inside of me.

Two fingers weren't enough.

As if he could sense my need, he slipped another finger inside me. I was stretched to the max, his fingers finding a rhythm that had me right on the edge.

My hips began moving in time with his thrusts, meeting each one. The back of the car was filled with the wet sound of Ford finger fucking me, and our shared, heavy breathing.

"That's it," Ford said. "Give it to me. Fuck me. I want you to come in my hand."

I gasped at his words, closing my eyes, head thrown back. I was close. So close.

Then Ford slid his thumb up, pressing against my clit.

"Mmm, God," I whimpered as my body clenched around his fingers, and I came harder than I ever had in my life. I was panting for air, riding out the waves of my orgasm, too caught up in the moment to even think about what was happening, or who it was happening with.

When I finally opened my eyes, Ford was wiping his hand on his jeans, a satisfied grin on his face.

"You were saying?" he asked, looking at me smugly.

I blushed, pulling my dress down, my pulse still sky high.

What the hell had Ford just done to me? It was a revelation. Nothing like before. A total fucking home run.

Not that I was going to say anything to him. He didn't need to know how new this was to me, how fucking incredible it had felt, how little experience I had to compare it to.

But there was no more hiding how much I wanted him.

Which meant I had to find a way to regain the upper hand.

As soon as possible.

EMZEE

CHAPTER 16

The Wives were deep in conversation when I arrived at The Gage for another Vault Lunch—unusual because Brooklyn was often the last one to show up—but it didn't take a genius to realize that they had to be deep in conversation about me.

When I got to the table, both their heads shot up, wearing identical smiles.

"Emzee!" Tori said. "Finally. We've been dying to hear what's going on."

They rose to greet me and we exchanged the usual round of hugs and cheek kisses.

Tori was wearing another one of her flowy maternity sundresses, stretching ever more tightly over her round belly. She always reminded me a little bit of a Disney princess, with her long blonde hair and big blue eyes.

Brooklyn's style was more edgy, but as a model, she always managed to look just a little more dressed up than everybody else—even on days like today, when she was in a pair of boyfriend jeans with black heels and a white button-up that was cuffed to the elbows.

I ran my hands down the front of my own jeans, feeling a little out of my league. But that's how I always felt around The Wives, even though I knew they'd be horrified to know it.

There was no doubt in my mind that both of them were dying for an update. Which I knew I owed them—I had a lot of explaining to do, obviously, considering that the last time we'd had lunch, I told them I was considering entering into a fake relationship with Ford. And now we were engaged.

The best course of action was probably perpetuating the big lie. Telling them they were right; that the relationship had started out fake but then became real...but I couldn't lie to them. Not when I so badly needed their help navigating the next fifteen months of falsely married bliss.

"How are you two?" I asked, trying to stall for time.

"We're not here to talk about us," Brooklyn said. "We're here for the details!"

"Time to spill," Tori added. "I've been waiting for this lunch date ever since you told us the happy news. At least, it sounded happy. Did some serious sparks start flying, or what?"

"I bet I know what started flying," Brooklyn teased.

My face got hot, and I grabbed a fried pickle from the plate on the table and stuffed it in my mouth, sliding down in my chair a little bit. "It's not what it looks like."

As if they could sense my hesitation, Tori leaned over and put a gentle hand on my arm.

"Sorry," she said. "We were being silly. Tell us everything. But also, no pressure."

Brooklyn nodded emphatically. "We just want to help."

The waitress arrived just in time to allow me a moment to collect myself, and after we'd ordered our lunches and I got half a glass of wine in me, I felt ready to give them the update they were clearly dying for.

I explained everything, getting them up to speed in a hurry by keeping it short and simple. There was Ford's fifteen-month plan, the way we'd sorted out the details, our end goal of keeping Ford's family off his back and his grandmother's ring off Claudia's finger. As for me, I'd be helping to repair some of the damage the Zoric family's reputation had undergone when my father had been arrested and the seedy underbelly of KZ Modeling had been revealed.

Tori and Brooklyn nodded along the whole time. Neither of them was a stranger to arranged marriages, we all knew that.

I did feel a little bad that I expected them to keep my secret from their husbands, but The Vault was The Vault, and all secrets shared at Vault Lunches were never to be repeated. Luckily, The Wives were fully on board with that. What my brothers didn't know wouldn't hurt them.

"I hate that you have to keep this from Stefan and Luka," I said. "I know it's not fair to expect you to lie to them."

It was honestly the thing I felt guiltiest about.

But both of them shook their heads.

"Don't worry about it," Tori said. "What goes in The Vault stays in The Vault."

Brooklyn agreed. "This is a sacred bond. We'd never betray it. Besides, we're excited."

"Just remember, this is all a show," I reminded them, pushing my ravioli aside. "I wouldn't get too excited."

The Wives exchanged a look.

"How often did I say that to myself?" Tori asked Brooklyn, who giggled.

"Probably about the same amount of times I did," she said.

"This is completely different," I argued.

"Uh-huh," Brooklyn said.

"Sure," Tori said.

The big grins on their faces indicated that they didn't think my situation was different at all. In fact, I was pretty sure they were more convinced than ever that my fake marriage would end up exactly the same way theirs had.

As real.

And truthfully, I didn't want to argue with them, especially because a part of my own heart was wishing for the same thing. As dumb as that was. And as dangerous.

"Now we have to discuss the most important thing," Tori said.

I frowned. "A prenup?" I asked tentatively.

"No!" Tori looked at Brooklyn. "The wedding!"

"Thank God," I said, letting out a sigh of relief. "That would actually be super helpful."

I was having a hard time getting anything figured out, beyond choosing a day to get the marriage license. Since the whole thing was a sham, there was no point in planning a big wedding, but I still felt overwhelmed by all the decisions I was supposed to make. Having my sisters-in-law volunteer for this was taking a huge weight off my shoulders.

"So where are you in the planning process?" Tori asked.

I told them that we'd set a date, two and half months away.

"Great, and what else?" Brooklyn prodded.

"That's it, really," I said. "I thought we'd have the ceremony outdoors, maybe the Morton Arboretum? Something simple. I'm not too worried about the details."

The Wives looked stricken.

"It's not real, remember?" I told them. "I don't want to make a big deal about this."

It turned out The Wives did not share my vision.

"Oh hell no," Brooklyn said, grabbing me by the shoulders and giving me a little shake. "Something simple? Not gonna work."

"You can't do simple," Tori said. "This is a huge deal! A marriage between two of the highest-powered families in Chicago? We have to go all out."

I didn't like the sound of that. "I just think that it'd be best if—"

"Besides, Em," Brooklyn said. "We never got to do this for ourselves, so this is our chance to make up for it. *We are planning our dream wedding for you.* No ifs, ands, or buts."

Tori nodded.

Well, wasn't this a big mess.

They both looked so happy with the prospect of planning the wedding that I didn't have the heart to tell them no. After all, they were right. A big wedding would help show all of Chicago that we were committed to each other and in love. It would legitimize the marriage and help repair my family's reputation, which was the real reason I was doing this.

Wasn't it?

"It's going to be a massive party, of course," Tori was saying.

"Anyone who's anyone will be invited," Brooklyn confirmed. "But the guest list will have to feel exclusive."

"The most anticipated event of the year," Tori agreed.

"It's in two and half months," I reminded them, but Tori waved me off.

"We have the money and the resources," she said. "We'll make it happen."

"Besides," Brooklyn added, "everyone will want to be involved in the wedding. It's great publicity."

I could see her eyes getting all starry. She was definitely picturing the wedding down to the last detail, her brain working to make the absolute picture-perfect moment for me and Ford.

"How involved do you think Ford will want to be?" Tori asked.

"In planning a wedding?" I raised my eyebrows. "I imagine he'd rather stick a red-hot poker in his eye than discuss table settings and color palettes."

The Wives laughed.

"Stefan was the same," Tori said. "Though my step-mother did most of the planning in the end. Thank God for Michelle."

"How are things going between you and Ford, by the way?" Brooklyn asked.

There was a suggestive tone to her voice that made it clear she wasn't asking about our contract negotiations.

"Fine," I said, even though I could feel my face heating up.

"*Just* fine?" Tori asked with the same tone.

"Have you done the deed yet?" Brooklyn pushed, never one to beat around the bush.

I thought about the other night, in the back seat of the car, Ford using his fingers and his voice to give me the hottest orgasm I'd ever had. Under the table, I squeezed my knees together, trying not to get distracted by the memories.

"No comment," I finally said, still blushing furiously.

Tori and Brooklyn were both studying me openly now.

"It hasn't happened yet," Tori finally guessed. "They're still tiptoeing around it."

I kept my mouth shut, knowing that if I disagreed, I'd just put fuel on the fire.

"Ahh." Brooklyn let out a dreamy sigh. "I remember that stage."

"I told you, this is different," I reminded them again. They were still convinced the sham would turn real before too long. "I'm not expecting anything real to happen with Ford."

Tori and Brooklyn nodded, their expressions kind but patronizing.

"Of course not," Tori said. "I certainly never expected anything real to happen between me and Stefan."

"Or me and Luka," Brooklyn said.

"It'll all work out," Tori says. "It just takes some time. And patience."

"I really don't think it's going to shake out that way just because it did for both of you," I said. "Ford and I have known each other for too long. He just sees me as a friend."

That was a lie, of course. He'd said that he was attracted to me, and he'd shown me very clearly what he would be capable of if we ended up in bed together. I had no doubt it would be amazing. But I also knew that his heart wasn't connected to his dick. He might want me, but he'd never love me. Not the way I loved him.

"Fake weddings are the new true love," Brooklyn said with a wink.

And that was that. Even if I could convince them the truth about my relationship with Ford, I knew they would continue to hope. Which wasn't helping me any.

To be honest, the whole thing was a lot of pressure. All the plans and the investment of their time and concern was weighing heavily on me. And what would happen when I had to let down everyone else with the news of my eventual divorce? The list of people I'd be disappointing seemed to be getting longer and longer by the day. Which was part of the reason I said, "I do have one request."

"Of course," Tori said. "Anything you want."

"No gifts. No physical gifts, at least. If people want to give us something, I'd like it to be a monetary donation to my charity."

"We can arrange that," Brooklyn said.

I let out a small sigh of relief. Even if everyone hated me at the end of this, at least some good would come out of it.

Leaning back in my seat, I couldn't ignore the sour feeling in my stomach. Was I engaging in the kind of justification that had led my father down the path to trafficking women? Women who were trying to earn their green cards with their bodies? Because it was starting to feel like it.

I could only pray that I wouldn't turn out anything like him.

EMZEE

CHAPTER 17

With The Wives moving full speed ahead planning my nuptials, I didn't have much to do except dive back into my usual routine. I knew there were things Tori and Brooklyn would need my feedback on—cake tasting, dresses, approving a caterer—but for the most part, they were thrilled to be handling all the details.

Meanwhile, Ford's mother's one stipulation was that the event be held at the Malone estate on Martha's Vineyard. If agreeing to a destination wedding would keep my future mother-in-law's nose out of the rest of the planning, I was more than happy to go along with it. The last thing I needed was extra wedding stress. I'd rather bury my head in the sand for the next two and half months and just focus on work.

That, and trying not to think about Ford and what he'd done to me in the back seat of the car.

Easier said than done, obviously.

I hadn't seen Ford since that night, but we had texted here and there over the last few days. He had a job that took up most of his waking hours, and his family liked to keep him busy as well. I expected we'd talk in more detail soon enough...after all, he couldn't do this whole fake marriage thing without me.

Even still, I was surprised when I received an email from him one morning. It wasn't his usual method of communication with me, and on top of that, it wasn't a regular email—it was unexpectedly formal, more like an invitation of some sort. And I was intrigued by all the specifics he outlined. What to wear (formal dress), where to meet (the Chicago Botanic Garden), when to be there. Yet he didn't give me a single hint as to what was actually supposed to happen.

So yeah, I was going to bite.

Knowing how much Ford had appreciated the Prada dress I wore to the ball, I had already bought another one in a soft blue shade more appropriate for daytime events (I wasn't going to be an outfit repeater just yet). So, on it went. It really made my gray eye color pop, and I was pretty sure Ford's jaw would drop when he saw me in it. Even with a pair of sensible flats and my black leather jacket over it, I looked totally smoking hot.

I left my hair down with just a touch of texturizing cream worked in, because I'd noticed the way he liked to play with it, but I took extra time with my signature winged eyeliner and kept the rest of my makeup simple. I felt good. Like myself. With all the lying and posing and dressing up for other people lately, it was nice to be comfortable in my skin again.

When I stepped out of my building to dial an Uber, I found a car ready and waiting for me at the curb.

That threw me. Ford had never been one for planning ahead, as evidenced by our entire spur-of-the-moment fake relationship, but apparently he was planning ahead tonight. It gave me a little thrill. I tried to give the driver directions, but he said that he knew where he was going. So I just leaned back into the plush leather seat and let myself be taken away.

The Chicago Botanic Garden was one of my favorite places in the city, and yet again, I was surprised that Ford had remembered. I'd definitely mentioned how much I loved shooting photos there, and I'd spent more than a few of my days off wandering around my favorite areas (the Aquatic Garden, the collection of tiny, perfect bonsai trees, the Japanese Garden), but I had never gotten the sense that Ford was paying much attention when I talked about it.

Suddenly, the evening seemed full of excitement and potential. It felt like Ford was making an effort. Like this might be a real date. My stomach immediately started tying itself in anxious little knots.

We hadn't spoken at all about what he'd done to me in the back seat of the car a few nights ago, but I knew that the dynamic between us had changed. I couldn't help wondering how—or if—it had affected him. If he had gone back to his apartment all keyed up and aroused afterward. I'd seen the bulge of his erection through his pants while he was fingering me, and it seemed that he hadn't been lying about how big his dick was.

Did he wear boxers or briefs? Or was he the type to go commando?

I could imagine him going commando. I liked imagining it.

In my fantasy, he had stretched out on his huge bed and pushed his pants down, out of the way, before gripping himself with a firm hand. Then he'd jerked off, hard and fast, thinking of how I'd come on his fingers. How I'd ridden his hand to a breathless orgasm in the back of a car, our driver mere inches away, separated from us by only a thin pane of glass. I imagined him coming with a groan, spurting all over himself, thinking about how wet he'd gotten me.

I fanned myself, suddenly overheating in my jacket, even with the sleeves pushed up to my elbows.

With a jolt, I realized that we had arrived. The driver pulled up to the entrance and then came around to open my door. As I slid out of the car, I thanked him, feeling my heart pound in anticipation. *Here goes nothing,* I silently told myself.

Walking into the gardens, I realized I was probably a little overdressed, but I was enjoying myself regardless. This place always felt so serene and peaceful, calm and cool, and the guests seemed to be thinning out as I headed deeper into the park. It had to be near closing time, as the park always shut down an hour or so before sunset, but nobody stopped me.

I made my way to the Aquatic Garden, where Ford had instructed me to meet him.

I was right on time.

The waterlilies were in bloom, but my attention was solely focused on Ford, who was standing on the boardwalk, waiting for me.

He looked edible.

Instead of his usual T-shirt and jeans, he had dressed up. A pair of charcoal pants perfectly tailored to fit his muscular thighs, with a matching vest and tie over a crisp blue shirt. Everything fit him like a dream, and his hair looked freshly cut. He'd shaved recently, too.

And in his hand a single orchid, *Masdevallia rolfeana*—a Costa Rican flower known for its deep, dark coloring. Not a true black, but a garnet color so deep that it was considered to be the only black orchid, it was my absolute favorite flower. Ford Malone had brought me one.

I had to admit, I was feeling a bit swoony.

Not only had he set up a real-ass date for us, but between the gussying up and the orchid, he'd clearly gone all out on his end as well. It was already the best date I'd ever been on.

My heart was literally throbbing in my chest as I approached him. Maybe he was giving this a real shot. Maybe after what happened the last time we were together, he'd been stirred enough to realize that—best friend or not—I was a woman, not just his longtime best friend, and that I deserved a little fake romance in our fake relationship. At least, a girl could hope.

The whole thing felt magical and surreal as I all but floated toward him.

"Wow, Em," he said. "You look...absolutely gorgeous."

He took my hand when I stopped in front of him and slid the orchid over my wrist—it was a corsage, I realized—then kissed the top of my knuckles gently. My knees went weak.

"Thank you," I murmured, smiling as I gazed up at him.

The sun was just beginning to set, spreading a warm glow over the gardens. Everyone had already left the area, so Ford and I were alone. Just as I was about to ask him what exactly he had planned for us, he dropped to one knee.

My heart flew up into my throat and my hands came up to my lips.

Was this...?

"Mara Rose Zoric," Ford said, on his knee in front of me. "Em. We've been friends for seven years, and we're soon to be a whole lot more. I simply cannot wait."

From his pocket, he pulled out a small square box. An unmistakably sized box.

"Ford..." I murmured, my voice catching in my throat.

He opened the box and there it was: his grandmother's antique ring. Two rows of the most perfect, beautiful little diamonds I'd ever seen, set in yellow gold, nestled against deep blue velvet. The ring sparkled in the fading sunlight, and for a moment I was speechless.

My eyes began to well up, the diamonds blurring.

"I know I should have done this before," Ford said. "I should have done something more official, but there's no reason I can't start now. Emzee, my nearest and dearest friend, will you marry me?"

It was the proposal of my dreams.

"I will," I said softly.

Ford slipped the ring onto my finger and stood. I thought, for a moment, that he'd take me into his arms and kiss me. Instead, he leaned back, and called out:

"She said yes!"

Immediately, Ford's friends began appearing from behind various trees and bushes, all cheering and applauding. It took me a moment to realize what was happening, but it all sunk in when I saw Mr. and Mrs. Malone, my brothers, and The Wives step out from behind a building.

"Congratulations!" everyone was saying.

They were all coming up to us, shaking Ford's hand, slapping him on the back, and pulling us into group hugs. I was so stunned that I didn't know what to say.

Ford had planned a whole goddamn surprise engagement party.

Yet again, everything was for show.

Like a fool, I had thought that this night was going to be about the two of us. But just like he'd done when we went out to dinner for that first time as a couple, only to end up meeting with his entire family, he'd put this whole romantic gesture together just for the optics. I felt sick.

Once again, my years of practice maintaining a poker face came in handy. It felt like I'd been using those skills a lot more recently. It was exhausting.

Tori and Brooklyn found me almost immediately, both wanting to see the ring.

"Oh, it's exquisite," Tori said, holding my hand up. "You love vintage. And it won't get in the way when you're working with your hands, either."

"It's absolutely perfect for you," Brooklyn agreed with a sigh.

My brothers came over to hug me as well, but being men, they didn't really have any comments about the ring.

"You look so beautiful," Tori said.

"Ford can't stop staring at you," Brooklyn noted. "I took tons of pictures already."

I turned to find that she was right—Ford was standing at the other end of the garden, talking to his friends, but his eyes were fixated on me. On the dress. When I caught his eye, he gave me a wicked smile and a wink.

Even though I was annoyed that he had once again played me, I couldn't help the thrill that ran through my body at his obvious attention. And I had to admit that he'd done everything right, at least as far as the whole "keeping up appearances" thing was concerned. Time to suck it up, make the small talk, and show off the ring like a good little fiancée would.

Even if I was seething all the while.

"Crab cake?" Tori asked.

A plate of canapés had been brought over to us, the waiters all dressed in suits and bow ties. I grabbed a crab cake and stuffed it in my mouth, though I barely tasted anything. The rest of the event seemed to pass in a blur.

None of it had gone how I had expected, and I was upset not just at Ford, but at myself. I couldn't believe I'd actually thought that he had changed. That our relationship had changed. When of course it hadn't. It was exactly the same as it had always been, where he made the decisions and expected me to go along with them, and I...well, I did.

Once again, Ford had successfully manipulated me.

And I just kept letting him.

Not anymore, I told myself, standing in the garden in my corsage and my dress, watching Ford make small talk in between bites of cocktail shrimp.

Soon enough, he was going to get an earful from me. Because I was going to make it perfectly clear to him that when it came to our fake engagement, he wouldn't be the only one calling the shots.

EMZEE

CHAPTER 18

I made it through the rest of the evening with a fake smile on my face, grinding my teeth to keep it there. Ford came over every so often, tucking his arm around my waist, lifting my hand so that our guests could examine and compliment the heirloom engagement ring he'd given me.

It really was perfectly subtle, especially since I'd never been the type of girl who wanted some huge rock on her finger. Even though I was still angry at Ford, I couldn't help admiring the ring every time I glanced down, appreciating the way the rows of antique diamonds sparkled in the moonlight and the glow of the candles that had been set up around the Aquatic Garden.

I loved the way it looked on my petite hand. Like it belonged there.

Not that I was going to tell Ford that.

He had to know I was pissed at him, because every time he'd put his hand around my waist and squeeze, I'd move away. Though obviously neither of us could comment on the tension. That would ruin the illusion of the happy, newly engaged couple.

And we couldn't have anything ruining the illusion.

So I played the good little fiancée for the rest of the evening, and I played it well. I smiled and made small talk and showed off the ring and gushed about how surprised I'd been.

"You looked utterly shocked," Ford's Aunt Miri—the one who had the excellent taste in Prada—said to me. "I've never been one to weep over romance, but I did get a little misty."

"I *was* shocked," I said. "Ford is amazing at surprises, aren't you, honey?"

He was beside me, and I could sense his hesitation. "I do try," he said with a chuckle.

"He's *so* good at it," I said, pouring it on thicker. "Always springing things on me out of nowhere. I never know what he's planning behind my back."

The words were pointed, and his smile faltered. But only briefly.

"Only because it's so much fun to surprise you," he said.

"I'll just bet it is," I said sweetly. "I'll have to surprise you myself one of these days."

At the end of the evening, as had become our pattern, Ford and I arranged to ride home in the same car so he could accompany me—purely for show, of course.

We were barely a few weeks into this charade, and I was already exhausted by it. Tired of the lies and the maneuvering that we were doing to convince people this was the real thing. I just wanted to go home and take off this dress and flop down on my bed and go to sleep. Thankfully, Munchkin's friendly dog walker had been by earlier to feed him and take him around the block, so I wouldn't have to do any of that when I got home.

Our car pulled up to the curb, and we got in, waving to our friends and family. I could see Tori and Brooklyn standing with my brothers, exchanging self-satisfied looks of "told you so." I wanted to tell them the truth—that what they'd witnessed between me and Ford earlier was a total sham, completely different from what they had with Stefan and Luka. That it wasn't going to end up the same way at all, because Ford was just manipulating me throughout this entire process. Whatever he wanted, he got, and I was hardly an afterthought.

As we turned onto the street, I scooted as far away from Ford as I could, moving to the other end of the back seat. He didn't say anything and didn't attempt to stop me, so he must have known how livid I was.

We spent the entirety of the car ride in silence. I was too riled up to say anything.

Instead, I kept looking out the window, trying not to think about how incredible and yet awful the evening had been, but I couldn't stop staring down at my lap, where the ring shone on my finger. I didn't want to keep admiring it, but my eyes kept getting drawn to its sparkly glory.

At one point, Ford cleared his throat, and I thought he was going to say something, but he remained silent. I was glad. I didn't want to get in a fight, and I needed some time to process everything. He knew I wasn't the kind of person who'd be into a surprise fake engagement party—had he played it close to the vest because he thought I wouldn't go along with it?

And all this after I'd been so clear with him about my expectations, about wanting to be kept in the loop.

Something else occurred to me then. When Ford had

gone down on one knee with that box in his hand, before our friends and family had popped out of the fucking shrubberies, I'd stupidly hoped for the *briefest* of moments that things between us had actually changed. What if he had kept the proposal a secret because he wanted it to mean something? Something real?

If so, what the hell? Was he into me that way or not? Was his attraction to me more than just physical? All the uncertainty was driving me bonkers. We definitely needed to have The Conversation, but first I had to get my head on straight.

Thankfully, we'd arrived at my apartment building.

I let Ford open the door for me, and then I swept myself out of the car and headed toward the entrance to my building without looking back. When I heard the car door close behind me, I expected to hear the car drive off next, and it took everything I had to keep from bursting into tears as I tried and failed to find my keys. But after the car had pulled away, I heard footsteps.

Turning around, keys still buried at the bottom of my purse, I found Ford standing there.

"What do you want?" I said icily.

"Can I come up?" he asked.

"You don't leave me much choice," I told him. "Your ride is already gone."

He held up his phone. "I can call him back," he said. "But I'd rather go up with you."

It was an unusual request, and it threw me off guard. I couldn't say no. "Fine."

I got the door open and he followed me through the lobby and into the elevator. The small space felt even smaller with him in it, and I kept my eyes focused on my shoes as the car made its way up to the loft floor.

When we walked into my place, I allowed myself to foolishly hope that Munchkin might attack Ford with a nice bite in the ass, but of course he didn't. Munchkin loved Ford, almost as much as he loved me. The two of them were thick as thieves. In fact, at this very moment, Munchkin was in Ford's arms, wagging that stub of a tail as Ford gave him a good ear scritch.

"Traitor," I muttered to my dog, dropping a kiss on the top of his head before swishing my way into the living room area and tossing my bag on the coffee table.

For a second I just stood there, wanting nothing more than to take off my dress and my shoes, my feet aching and my entire body exhausted by the past several hours. But it would have to wait. I was most assuredly not taking off a single article of clothing as long as Ford fucking Malone was standing there.

As if sensing my impatience, Ford put my dog down. Munchkin took off for my bedroom, probably to jump up and take a nap on the cushy mattress while he knew I was too distracted to kick him off. Meanwhile, Ford ran his hand through his hair and looked at me.

"I'm sorry, Em," he said, finally breaking the ice. "I should have warned you."

"Mm-hmm," I grunted. I was surprised at the apology but didn't show it, crossing my arms over my chest instead. No way in hell was I going to forgive him that easily.

"You're my first fake fiancée," Ford continued, trying for a conspiratorial smile. "It's all new to me. I don't know what I'm doing, and I fucked up."

It wasn't what I had been expecting.

Still, it wasn't enough.

"Yeah, well, this doesn't feel anything like the partnership we discussed when you do things like that," I said, letting all my anger boil over. "What were you even thinking?"

He seemed a little taken aback by my passion, but he didn't try to talk me down, just stood there and listened.

"We're supposed to be a team," I railed, venting the frustration I'd been holding in all night long. "I agreed to do this for *you*—yes, there are some benefits to my family, but the whole reason we're in this mess is because you can't stand up to your parents."

"That's fair," Ford said, looking properly deflated. "And I get it. Honestly. I understand. I wasn't thinking at all."

"No, you fucking weren't."

I knew I was being unduly harsh, but I didn't care.

"Seeing you get down on one knee with a box in your hand, when I thought it was just the two of us," I went on, "I didn't know what to make of it. Especially after what happened the other night, in the car..." I trailed off, embarrassed at what I was admitting. That for a second, I'd actually believed his proposal might mean something.

I hadn't meant to bring up our hookup in the car, either, but it was out now and there wasn't anything I could do about it.

"You're right about all of it," Ford said, stepping closer to me. "I made it confusing. I know. So how about I un-confuse things?" He took my hands in his. "The fake stuff is the fake stuff—the proposal, the wedding, the farce. That's all for show."

He moved even closer to me and I could feel his breath hot on my cheeks.

"But what happened in the car?" he said, his voice dropping lower. "That was real."

"It was?" I asked, hating how uncertain I sounded.

"Yes," he said, tucking my hair behind my ear. "Let me show you exactly how real."

I swallowed hard as he led me over to the couch. He gestured for me to sit, and I did.

Then he knelt down. He didn't have a ring this time, but my heart was pounding as fast as it had when there'd been a velvet box in his hand. My whole body was tingling, and it was getting hard to breathe as I waited for him to show me what he'd promised.

His hands started at my feet, pulling my shoes off one at a time. The fabric of my dress was cool against my legs, but underneath it my entire body ached for Ford. For his touch.

He slipped his hands underneath the hem of my dress, slowly, carefully sliding it up to my thighs. Then his fingers trailed their way back down to my knees, and he pushed them apart, so suddenly that I gasped. And I let him. In fact, I helped him, lifting my hips up as his hands traveled to the waistband of my silky black thong.

"I love knowing you were barely wearing anything under this dress," he said as he drew the underwear down my thighs, letting them drop to the floor. I kicked them aside, keeping my legs open for him and bunching my skirt up at my waist. I should have felt exposed, but I didn't.

"This is nice," Ford said.

He'd just gotten a glimpse of my trim landing strip. I liked being mostly bare, and I could tell from his expression that he liked it too.

He spread my legs even wider, making the muscles of my inner thighs burn a little at the tension. At first, I was expecting to feel the brush of his fingers, assuming he was going to do exactly what he'd done in the car the other night. My body was ready and wet, eager for it, but then, instead of using his hands, Ford lowered his head and tasted my pussy.

I cried out at the shock of his hot tongue lapping against my lips, tracing a line from bottom to top, around my clit, and back down again. My head fell back against the couch cushions, my hands clenching the fabric of my dress as Ford began to fuck me with his tongue.

No one had ever done anything like this to me.

It was so good.

Ford stopped and pressed his tongue against my clit, sucking it softly into his mouth, and then the low moan he let out vibrated through my entire body.

"Oh my God," I groaned, panting for air. I was breathing so hard I worried I was going to pass out, but if I did, it would be worth it. "Fuck...yes..."

Pleasure washed over me in wave after wave as he licked and sucked and caressed me with his tongue. I was so wet, so dripping wet for him, but he seemed to like it, nuzzling his chin against my inner thighs before returning to drag his tongue against my slit. God, his tongue. Strong and sure and steady, lapping up and down, darting right inside my pussy, thick and wet. So fucking good.

I was moaning now, an orgasm rapidly building. It had never felt this way before, not even when I was alone with my vibrator. I panted as Ford parted me and slid one finger deep inside of me, keeping his mouth over my clit, sucking it like a Hoover. I was riding his hand now, grinding hard against his fingers and mouth, seeking the relief that I knew was close.

"I'm going to come," I panted, squeezing my eyes shut.

My toes curled into the carpet, my body arching up and away from the sofa as Ford inserted another finger in my pussy. I loved the way his body stretched mine, the way I could feel his fingers moving inside me, matching the quick, hard rhythm of his tongue on my clit.

He began to move faster, harder, coaxing the climax out of me, and my body responded.

"I'm coming, I'm coming, I'm coming," I whimpered, pleasure arching through me as I came—so fucking hard, I couldn't believe another person had done this to me, moaning so loud, I wondered if my neighbors could hear it. But Ford didn't stop until I finally pushed him away, falling back breathlessly against the couch, my entire body buzzing.

He stood, and I could tell he was aroused, the hard press of his cock evident against the zipper of his pants. I half expected him to sweep me up into his arms and carry me to the bedroom, to finish what we had started.

Instead, he leaned down and gave me a kiss on the forehead.

"I should go," he said. "I'll call you."

Somehow I managed to nod, laying there in a daze as Ford let himself out. It wasn't until I heard the door click closed that I realized exactly how much trouble I was in.

I was screwed, and I knew it.

Figuratively, since Ford was such a damn good lover and my heart was bound to get attached...but I was also pretty sure I'd be getting literally screwed soon enough as well.

Because there was no way I was going to be able to resist him.

And I knew my heart wouldn't be able to, either.

EMZEE

CHAPTER 19

E ven though my brain and body were in complete disagreement regarding what to do about my fake fiancé, I was able to push that debate aside as I headed out of my apartment the next day. It was my absolute favorite day of the month—my teaching day.

Since I had founded See Yourself, I'd discovered that my passion for photography was only rivaled by my love of teaching it. It was my greatest joy to run an organization where I could help former KZM models move forward with their lives. Offering photography classes through the nonprofit was just one way I was able to do that.

Initially, when the allegations about KZ Modeling had come out, I'd been devastated. I hadn't wanted to believe my father could do something as fucked up as trafficking women to be sex slaves under the cover of the agency, and of course I'd been shielded from his illicit activities for my entire life. But as the evidence mounted and more women came forward, it became impossible to deny what he'd done. The gravity of his betrayal. The lives he'd ruined.

Once he was locked up in jail, and my initial shock had

worn off, I realized I wanted to do something to help the women my father had hurt.

That's how See Yourself had been born. It was my humble attempt to start making amends for my father's crimes. My nonprofit helped former KZM models leave behind the seedy side of the industry, where modeling and prostitution had gone hand in hand, and gave them a safe, supportive place to learn about different careers and gain job skills.

See Yourself fostered recovery by offering a sense of community, providing counseling and employment agency referrals, and holding workshops and seminars to help the women discover new career paths. So far I'd hosted executives from cosmetics companies, wedding photographers, staffing specialists, even the owner of a local bakery. But my photography classes were always locked in on the schedule —they formed the core curriculum of the charity.

I liked having a chance to use my extremely expensive art school education to do good. Because the truth was, these women had essentially paid for my college education. The work they had done on their backs had funded my father's lifestyle, and therefore mine as well. Now, my charity was a chance to pay it forward to the people who had made my privileged life possible. It felt like the very least I could do.

Days like today were spent at the charity's space, a beautiful studio in the Loop (not too far from Danica Rose Management) that we rented to hold classes. I'd started my day by teaching a basic skills class in the morning. See Yourself provided all its students with cameras and simple equipment, as well as time in a local photo developing lab, but they still needed someone to walk them through all the basic beginner-level stuff. I loved getting to see a batch of budding new photographers learn exactly how powerful an image could be, and how it was possible to create something powerful themselves.

Not all of my students ended up being as enamored with photography as I was, but the ones who did usually "graduated" from the initial classes onto the next level, which was more of a one-on-one mentoring program with me. After that, I'd use my connections to try to find them jobs, but regular employment was a challenge for anyone pursuing a career in the arts.

"Hi, Emzee!" a voice called across the studio as I sat waiting for my mentees to arrive.

"Galina!" I replied, jumping out of my seat. "Did you bring me your latest assignment?"

Though I tried my best not to play favorites amongst my students, I'd grown particularly fond of Galina, one of the models my father had trafficked from Bulgaria. She was passionate about photography and had exhibited a true talent for it, thanks to her natural eye for light and composition. I thought she could really make a place for herself in the photography world if she just had the right training and connections.

Luckily, those were two things that I could provide.

"I am not sure how they have worked," she said, holding an envelope close to her chest.

Holding out my hand, I smiled gently. "Let's find out then, yeah? If you're not happy with the images, you can always give it another go."

Honestly, I expected her photos to be great. I was always excited to see everything she brought me. This month, all my mentees had been instructed to shoot a series of self-portraits. I had been impressed with the vision and variety I'd seen so far, but I was especially interested in

Galina's work. She always had such an interesting perspective on the assignments I gave.

"Okay," she said, tentatively handing over the envelope.

Despite telling her multiple times how blown away I was by her work, she still seemed hesitant about taking too much pride in it. I got the sense that she didn't necessarily trust that the work was good, when in fact—in my professional opinion—it was very, very good.

"Maybe we can talk about what you think is and isn't working, and then we'll figure out how you can address those things on the next assignment. Cool?"

"Cool." Galina nodded, her teeth nibbling her bottom lip.

She was one of the more striking models my father had signed. A big part of the notoriety of KZ Modeling—besides the illegal prostitution aspect of it—had been that the agency's models were purported to be the most beautiful in the world.

Galina was a perfect example of that.

She had a regal face with incredible cheekbones and a full, wide mouth, perfectly balancing out her broad forehead, while thick, shining black hair fell down to her shoulders. Her skin was a dusky golden hue, and her eyes were a shade of blue that contrasted sharply with her dark features. On top of that, she had the kind of long, effortlessly lean body type that looked amazing in designer clothes. It was no wonder she had been so popular with both types of KZ Modeling clients. She was absolutely stunning.

"Here we go," I said, smiling as I started to spread her images across the long table by the window. There were eight of them, which was a good number—most students turned in about five to seven per assignment, though I allowed them to bring up to ten of whichever photos they thought were the strongest in the series.

Usually, however, I'd see a bunch of slightly different versions of essentially the same photograph—they tended to have a specific vision in mind and wanted my help choosing the image that best illustrated what they were trying to convey. This was how they built up their portfolios over the course of their mentorship.

Galina, though? She always tackled her assignments differently. That's why I enjoyed working with her so much. Her images always told a story, not with an individual image, but via a series of them. This was why, even though all of my students were passionate and talented, she struck me as the most inclined toward a career as a professional photographer. Maybe not even in fashion, but in photojournalism. She was that talented. With a little guidance and a broader education, she could be out there in the field, shooting some truly amazing images.

That's what I wanted for her. I wanted her life to be better because of me. To counter how it had been worse because of my father.

Once I had laid out all eight images in a neat row, I took a step back to observe them all together. They were stunning.

"Galina," I said. "These are incredible."

She had been looking nervous, but immediately brightened at my praise.

"They are?" she asked.

"They are," I said, before turning my full attention back to the work she'd brought.

The series of self-portraits began with her fully clothed in her brightly lit apartment. With each photograph, the light began to fade, as more of her body was exposed. The final image was taken with only moonlight for illumination, revealing enough of her bare skin that you could tell she was nude, though most of the light fell on Galina's face. She had purposely worn the same expression for the whole series—a strong, unflinching stare, directly into the camera.

"Gorgeous," I murmured.

Together, the images seemed to tell a very specific story. One about sex and sensuality. About Galina's ownership of her body and her control over how she wanted it to be seen.

Not only had the series required a tremendous amount of thought, planning, and skill for it to work as well as it did, but it was beautifully shot and extremely powerful. I felt my eyes welling up just looking at the images again, and I cleared my throat, trying to compose myself.

"Is...is it okay?" Galina asked, noticing my reaction.

"It's magnificent," I told her, honestly. I was completely choked up. "This is the best work I've seen from you."

Her face brightened. "It is?"

"Absolutely," I said. "I'm so proud of you."

She blushed, but seemed thrilled with the praise.

"I love the story you're telling," I said. "It seems to be a statement about the power you have, over your own body and your sexuality."

"Yes. I try to show myself in the pictures. But only what I want to show, not all of me."

We'd never really spoken about the horrors she had endured working for my father, but it seemed like we were speaking about it now. And while I didn't tend to address the elephant in the room very often with my students, the photos were almost like an invitation.

"Sex must be complicated now," I said gently. "After everything you've been through."

To my surprise, Galina shook her head. "Actually, no. It is not so difficult at all."

"Really?"

"Really," she said, smiling. "When you choose it for yourself, it can be very fulfilling still." She pointed to the pictures. "That is what I mean to say here. The lights, the way they go dim—for me, they are a symbol. Of creating the...the mystery that comes with not knowing how a new body responds to yours. And then the discoveries, of all the senses, that come with moving from the day to the night."

"Wow. That's...I don't know what to say," I murmured. "This is so good to hear."

She reached for me, putting a hand on my shoulder. "Please do not think I am unable to experience pleasure simply because I once put men's needs and pleasure before mine. It is all about the choice, and...being able to choose. That is pleasure."

I nodded, taking in her words.

We discussed the images for the rest of our session, working together to find ways to improve upon something that was already practically perfect. I was so proud of the work, and eager to see what she would come up with for the next assignment, which was to photograph a place that was meaningful to her. I knew she'd do something completely unexpected.

Galina never failed to surprise me. Not just with her work, but the thoughtfulness with which she composed her shots and the metaphorical meanings they contained. She always spoke so eloquently about her intentions, and her words about sex and sensuality stuck with me all day, through the rest of my classes, and even through my ride home that afternoon.

Even when I got back to my apartment and took

Munchkin for his walk around the neighborhood, I found that I was still thinking about what Galina had said. How her past experiences with sex hadn't destroy her sexuality or desire for pleasure. How for her, it was about choice.

Her words kept turning over in my head, even after I decided against ordering take-out and poured myself a glass of wine. I couldn't stop thinking about her photographs and her explanation behind them. Even when I curled up on my couch and tried to read the new Mapplethorpe biography, I found that my mind kept wandering back to sex. Sex and choice.

I hadn't really thought about it in that way. And now I couldn't stop thinking about it. Couldn't stop thinking about the choice that I had.

Finally, I gave up pretending that I could focus on anything but the idea that I was going to choose for myself as well.

I wanted Ford.

And despite everything that had happened between us with the fake engagement, I trusted him. I also knew that he knew exactly what he was doing, exactly how to give me pleasure. I knew he would make it feel good for me.

He was going to be my first.

It was my choice.

Not that he needed to know that it would be my first time. He just needed to want me back. Which I was confident that he did.

Decision firmly made, I took out my phone and texted Ford. *Dinner tonight? Just the two of us. Pick someplace you love.*

He responded quickly, probably seeing this as his chance to make amends for the surprise proposal fiasco.

As my lady requests, he texted. *I also have some ideas*

about how to secure additional funding for your charity, if you're interested.

I almost asked him to come over right on the spot. Nothing was hotter to me than Ford offering to help with my charity. Instead, I just said I would see him soon and leaned back against the couch cushions, preparing for my last several hours as a virgin.

EMZEE

CHAPTER 20

Everest, the world-renowned French restaurant in the Chicago Stock Exchange, had one of the most beautiful views in the city. We were treated like royalty there, which I suppose wasn't too far from reality; the Malones were revered by locals in the know. The fact that Ford had managed to secure us a table on such short notice proved exactly how well-respected his family was.

Chicago glittered below us as we dined on a menu of flawless dishes that were an instant aphrodisiac for a foodie like me: perfectly seared sea scallops, fresh Maine lobster with smoked bacon and maize bisque, Caspian Sea caviar, carnaroli risotto with forest mushrooms. Each plate came with its own pairing of wine, so by the time our dessert of decadent caramel tarte tatin came around, I was feeling warm and relaxed and happy.

Ford had gone all out. Beyond the meal, his undivided attention was focused on me the entire time. We barely talked about our fake engagement, or the increasingly stressful upcoming wedding—instead, it was like old times. He had me get him up to speed on See Yourself, and I spent some time describing the classes I'd taught earlier that day. Then he filled me in on his fundraising ideas and offered to pass around some of my students' resumes at the Malone Real Estate Holdings office, since his company regularly hired photographers to shoot new property listings. We discussed Tori and Brooklyn and my upcoming position as Auntie Em and gushed about how much we both still loved our hometown of Chicago, all while perched above its sparkling beauty, enjoying some of the best food the city had to offer.

It was magical.

We stayed at the restaurant until closing, and then, instead of taking a car back to my apartment, Ford suggested we walk the mile and a half since the weather was so mild.

Even though I had no intention of letting the date end when we got to my front door, I was enjoying our night out together and happy to walk off some of my fullness. By the time we reached my block, most of the tipsy feeling from the wine had faded. I was clearheaded, and as resolute as ever about my decision to invite Ford upstairs.

Even still, as we walked up the pathway to my building's entry doors, I was buzzing from the inside with anticipation. My hands were shaking a little, but I smoothed them down the front of my dress to hide my trembling. I was wearing a simple black sheath that clung to my curves, and had opted for a pair of sequined black designer flats for our date, which meant the top of my head barely reached Ford's biceps as we walked side by side. Still, I was glad I hadn't gone for the stilettos I'd been debating, or our walk home would have been a lot less fun.

"Come up," I told Ford when we got inside the lobby.

There was a question in his eyes, but he didn't verbalize

it. My request wasn't that unusual—we'd gone out to plenty of dinners that were followed by drinks at my place—though the late hour was a bit out of the ordinary, as were the distinctly date-like vibes of the evening.

We were both silent as we rode the elevator up to my loft, and the whole car seemed to crackle with tension, though I couldn't tell if it was mutual or just me imagining things.

The second we stepped into my loft, Munchkin greeted Ford by running around him in circles, panting excitedly. It seemed that we were in agreement about Ford staying the night.

I just wished I knew how to proceed.

Ford sat on the bench in the kitchen area, leaning down to scratch Munchkin as I poured us two glasses of water.

"I need to take him out, actually," I said, nodding at my dog. "You tired from our walk over here, or are you up for another lap around the block?"

"I'm not tired at all," he said. Maybe he was secretly as keyed up as I was.

We headed back out, walking in silence. I felt it again, that tension between us. Like a taut wire, just waiting to snap. I had to quit stalling. It was now or never.

Time to make my move.

"So. The real stuff and the fake stuff you talked about," I began. "What was tonight?"

"What do you mean?"

I shrugged. "When you offered to help with the charity, and the funding, or when you mentioned finding jobs for the women...was any of that real for you? Or did you just get carried away with the fantasy of being the perfect fake fiancé? And the dinner date—was that real?"

Ford stopped, turning to face me.

171

"It was real, Em," he said. "Everything tonight was real. And my feelings about the charity, too—about the photos you described Galina shooting—all of it. I really was moved by the whole thing and I'm glad to be a part of it in any way I can. Now and always."

As he was speaking, Munchkin, who had already finished his business, was leaning up against Ford's leg, getting scritched into full submission.

Okay. Done deal. I was his.

Ford's words were exactly what I needed to hear. All my hesitations, my nerves, were washed away. He was a good man, the right man. And I trusted him like nobody else.

"How about a proper nightcap?" I said. I wasn't ready to let him go. Neither was Munchkin, clearly.

"I'd love that," he said, but I could tell by the look in his eyes that he knew a drink wasn't the real reason I was inviting him up.

My hands started shaking again as we reached my front door for the second time in less than twenty minutes, but the moment we stepped inside, Ford was on me.

He pinned me against the door, his mouth hot and hard against mine.

I sighed with pleasure, dropping Munchkin's leash. Vaguely I heard the sound of the dog's nails tapping across the kitchen floor and disappearing into the plush living room where I was certain that he was settling down in his bed. It was late, so he would likely curl up and go right to sleep.

But I wasn't tired at all. I'd never felt more alive.

With Ford's lips against mine, I felt like I was waking up...like my body was waking up.

Ford's hands were everywhere—in my hair, against my

hips, sliding down to grip my ass. He was firm and confident and I loved it. Loved that he knew exactly what he was doing and that I had no doubts about what I was doing. I wanted him so bad I could hardly stand it.

His mouth moved from my lips, down my throat, kissing and nipping as he went, leaving little sparks of pleasure as I gasped. His grip was tight in my hair and it hurt a little, but in the best possible way. I'd never known kissing could be like this.

It wasn't that I had zero experience, of course, but I knew without a doubt that Ford was different from the other men I'd hooked up with. That this would be a world apart.

It would be better. It would be incredible. We were already so connected.

I knew I'd made the right choice before our clothes had even begun to come off.

Ford and I stumbled down the hallway, kissing even more deeply as we went, his tongue exploring every corner of my mouth as his hands stroked every part of my body through my dress. I was on fire, and I could feel exactly how much he wanted me, too.

His cock was straining against his pants, pressing against my belly. I could tell he was huge, and I silently prayed that he would feel good to me, that we would fit together just right.

With complete ease, Ford lifted me up, my arms circling his neck, my legs wrapping around his hips. His hardness pushed even more firmly against me, and I couldn't help grinding my hips into him, drunk on the feeling of his cock, so ready for me and so close. Despite my anxiety, the pleasure I felt being near him, his body against mine, overrode everything else.

"I want you," I panted into his mouth.

Groaning, Ford carried me, never breaking our kiss, into my bedroom.

It was dark, the only illumination being the moonlight streaming in through my window. It made the whole thing seem romantic and dreamlike, much like the whole evening had been.

Ford tossed me down on the bed as if I weighed nothing. I reached out my arms, wanting him to follow me, but he stood at the edge of the bed, looking down at me. I was suddenly paranoid about my likely state of disarray: my ravaged hair, my streaked eyeliner, my—

"You're beautiful," he said, melting all my worries away.

I shivered from the pleasure of his words, the husky sound of his voice.

"So are you," I said, taking in the familiar, perfect angles of his face, his broad shoulders, his tall, well-built body. Everything I wanted.

He laughed, and then his smile turned wicked.

"What are you wearing under that dress?" he asked. "Are you wearing good-girl panties, or a bad-girl thong?"

I looked up at him, my heart pounding. "Why don't you look and find out?"

His grin grew even more wicked.

"I think I will," he said, climbing up the bed, up my body, until his lips met mine again.

As he did, his hand found my thigh, and he began to push the hem of my dress up my leg, while his mouth moved to my ear, catching my earlobe between his teeth with exactly the right amount of pressure.

I felt his hand moving up, that confident slide of his hot palm. Finally he found what he was looking for, the roughness of his fingers brushing against my most intimate part.

Ford froze. "Are you wearing nothing underneath this dress?" he demanded.

I gave him a grin of my own.

"You naughty, naughty girl," he said.

He shoved my knees apart, finding my already wet opening with astonishing speed. Then he stroked my outer lips first, circling with his thumb. I could feel my pleasure building even before he slipped a finger inside of me, and then another, stretching my body deliciously. This was how it had been in the back of the car and I responded in the same way, my hips jerking as he began fucking me with his fingers. God, he was good with his hands.

Bright lights started swimming in front of my eyes and I reached for his hand, gently easing his fingers aside. I wasn't ready to come yet. Not like this.

"I want you," I told him for the second time, meeting his gaze. "*All of you.*"

I hoped he understood what I was saying, but before I could clarify further, Ford was kissing me again, working my dress up my hips with one hand while unzipping me with the other. In seconds, the dress was over my head. I was naked beneath him, heart pounding anew. The look on his face made me glad I'd decided not to wear anything under the dress.

"Look at you," he said, his eyes grazing my entire body. "You're fucking perfect."

I could feel myself blushing. I'd always been self-conscious about the size of my breasts, how big they were in proportion to the rest of me, especially in comparison to most of the women who modeled for Danica Rose. And I was definitely a lot curvier than Claudia.

But now, with Ford staring at me like a dessert he wanted to lap up, I felt sexy, powerful, and maybe—like he'd said—perfect for him. Propping myself up on my elbows and arching my back, I gave him an even better view.

"Fuck," he said, filling his hands with my breasts.

I felt like I was on the verge of an orgasm again, just from the way his fingers grazed and tweaked my overly sensitive nipples. When he lowered his hot mouth to capture one between his teeth, I caught my breath. It felt so good, the way he lavished them with attention, sucking and teasing each one in turn, his straining cock pressing between my naked hips.

"Ford," I moaned in a half whisper.

He was still fully dressed. Unacceptable. As he played with my nipples, I used my remaining strength to get his shirt off and then pressed my palms to his bare chest, relishing the feel of his firm pecs, the ridges of his six-pack, the fine dusting of hair below his belly button, until my fingers reached the edge of his waistband, his belt, his zipper. I paused, breathing hard.

This was it.

Taking my pause as an invitation, Ford lifted off the bed to shed the rest of his clothes.

I was grateful for the darkened room, hoping it hid the fact that my jaw nearly dropped to the floor. His cock wasn't just big, it was...well, it was gorgeous. Perfectly proportioned. And perfectly hard. I had no idea how it was going to fit. Suddenly, I was nervous all over again.

"Wait," I said.

Even though I had made my decision, I didn't know what to do regarding the matter of my inexperience. It would probably be better if I told Ford that I was a virgin, but I was also worried that the knowledge would be too much for him—that he'd realize I had Feelings for him, and then decide we shouldn't go through with it.

"You okay?" Ford asked, sitting on the edge of the bed. "We can stop."

Even in the moonlight, I could see the concern in his eyes, the questions there.

"No! I—I just wanted to make sure you had a condom," I said.

Ford gave me that devastatingly handsome grin of his.

"Of course," he said, digging a foil packet out from his pile of clothes.

I watched as he rolled it on, the thin latex stretching over his impressive length. Once he was sheathed, he pressed himself against me again, his body hot and heavy above mine, his tongue sliding deep into my mouth.

I kissed him back eagerly, my body tingly and taut and electric. I knew I was soaking wet, I could feel it, and Ford slipped a hand between our bodies, letting out a groan of appreciation when he slipped a finger back inside me.

"You're going to feel amazing around my cock," he said. "So hot. So wet."

I didn't respond, just let myself focus on the feel of his mouth and his body as his cock nudged against my entrance. I tried to relax, spreading my legs wide, looking into Ford's eyes in the dark, feeling his lips curve into a smile against mine.

Then he pushed inside me, in one sure, deep thrust.

I bit my lip as I cried out, and then Ford was moaning along with me as he started to move. We were kissing again, both of us making soft sounds, the moment between us— after all these years—so completely unbelievable and yet so right all at the same time. It was happening. I was having sex. With Ford. And it was amazing and incredible and maybe a little uncomfortable too, but it wasn't the kind of pain that hurt, it was the kind that felt good.

It was also different from how it had been with my vibrator inside me, better, hotter, but I also knew that my active self-love practices had prepared my body for this, and I was glad.

"Fucking hell," Ford groaned, picking up the pace. "You feel so fucking good. Such a tight fucking pussy."

His words made me even hotter. Wetter.

I moved with him, and we found a rhythm, straining against each other, chasing our own pleasure as we gave ourselves to each other. It wasn't uncomfortable anymore. It was exactly what I wanted, Ford pumping harder and faster, me trying to take all of him inside me, connecting with him on this new level we'd never experienced together before.

His hips drummed against mine, and then he was wrapping my legs around his waist, the new angle helping him sink even deeper inside. We groaned together at the pleasure.

"God, you're hot," Ford said. "So hot and tight."

I loved the words he was whispering in my ear as he fucked me. It was just one more way he was getting me off, beyond the miracle of his body and my emotional ties to him.

"So good," I murmured, my fingers digging into his shoulders. "You feel so good."

Most of the goodness, I knew, was because it was Ford. The man I'd loved for so long. He might not feel the same about me, but maybe he did. It felt like he did. And not just because he knew exactly what my body wanted. It was more than that. Our connection was so much deeper than just being friends, even Ford couldn't have denied that.

His strokes started getting slower and out of sync, his grunts louder, and I realized he was starting to approach his climax before he even told me, roughly, "I want you to come first."

Rolling onto his back and taking me with him, I suddenly found myself on top of Ford, his cock thrusting up inside me at a whole new angle. His hands went to my hips and he gripped me tight, pushing and pulling me back and forth over his length. Even still, I was in control of how deep he was, how fast, how hard. My hips moved in time, pleasure flooding my body as I rode him, my orgasm building to a crescendo with every passing second.

"Oh my God. More. More," I moaned, head tilting back as his thrusts sped up again.

"Fuck, I want to feel you come," he nearly growled, shifting his hand so his thumb was pressing against my clit as I fucked him.

Every stroke was pleasure, agony, sweet and hot, sending sparks from my clit to my toes.

"Ford," I panted, my voice trembling. "Ford, fuck, oh fuck—"

I leaned forward onto his chest, clinging to his shoulders, burying my face in his neck as I started to slip over the edge. It was happening. I was coming hard, so hard, moaning uncontrollably as the orgasm rippled through me, stronger and deeper inside than I had ever experienced before. I could feel my pussy clenching tight around him with every contraction of sheer, pulsing ecstasy, and I knew he felt it too because he let out a groan and suddenly he was slamming into me, wild and fast, cursing and whispering my name as he found his own release.

"Em," he moaned, the sound making me shiver even as I started to recover.

Our bodies were tangled as we caught our breath, our hearts racing in time, our skin slick with sweat. I didn't want it to be over, so I shifted onto my side next to him, my body in a position more comfortable for both of us, and rested my head on his chest.

I'd done it. I'd had sex. With Ford Malone.

The man I'd always loved.

And in that moment, I realized there was no point in worrying that I would lose my heart to him. Because I accepted the truth: that I already had. A long, long time ago.

FORD

CHAPTER 21

I, Ford Malone, was not a cuddler. Never had been. Not even with Claudia, after all our years together, though she hadn't been especially cuddly either.

But for the first time in my rich, varied, and satisfying sexual history, I found myself lingering after the act. Usually, once I'd finished, I was out of the bed, out of my partner's arms and in the bathroom. Getting rid of the condom and planning my escape route—either right out the door or at least out of the room.

So it surprised me that after fucking Emzee, I stayed in the bed way longer than I was accustomed to. Even if it was only a few minutes afterward. Not my usual MO at all.

The sex had been incredible. She'd been so hot and so incredibly tight that it had taken almost all my energy and focus not to come the moment I was inside her. She had felt so good, still felt so good, that I was reluctant to remove myself from her arms.

I could still hear the sharp gasps of pleasure she'd made as she came on my cock, her whole body tightening around me in the most unimaginable bliss. I knew if I kept thinking about it, I'd get hard again.

Truthfully, I hadn't been expecting our chemistry to be so out of control.

Emzee's head was still resting on my chest, one of her thighs thrown casually across my hips. It felt good. Almost like she belonged there. But I couldn't afford to think like that.

Slowly I pulled away, half expecting her to continue clinging to me, but she didn't. Mumbling something in a half-asleep daze, she rolled over in the bed, in all her gorgeous, naked glory. She was the very picture of a woman satisfied.

I felt a twinge of guilt for sneaking away, which, of course, was ridiculous. The last thing I needed was for her to get even more emotionally tangled up with me. I knew it was inevitable to a certain extent, what with our upcoming fake marriage—and especially after having sex—but I didn't want to encourage it. She'd get the picture soon enough.

"Where you going?" she asked, apparently awake enough to realize I was heading for the door.

"Bathroom," I said, easing the door shut slowly enough to catch her waving a dreamy hand before letting it fall back onto the bed, as if it had taken her last bit of energy to do so.

I felt a swelling of masculine pride as I headed down the hall to wash up and get rid of the condom. It wasn't until I turned the bathroom light on that I noticed the blood. Not a lot, just a small smear on the condom.

I stared at it for a moment. It wasn't enough blood for a period, I knew that. Instead, it was just enough...

Shit.

Emzee had been a virgin.

I'd just taken that from her.

She had *given* it to me.

I got rid of the condom and leaned against the sink, my thoughts spinning.

Sure, I'd known that she was a little inexperienced when it came to long-term relationships and the level of intimacy that entailed...but I had *never* imagined that she was a virgin. Of course, now that I took a moment to think about it, it made perfect sense. Emzee had never had a boyfriend in high school, not with all the bullying she'd gone through, and although she had started dating once she went away to college, it had never been anything serious.

In fact, all of her relationships had really been more like...flings. Not just in terms of how long they lasted (or didn't last, actually), but in the way she talked about the guys, as if she was happy enough to have a little fun with them, but only up to a certain point. Maybe the point where they wanted to go all the way, and she decided they weren't good enough.

And no wonder. She had a bad habit of choosing real losers.

She also had never struck me as the kind of girl who would usually engage in no-strings-attached sex, so it made sense that she had waited. In a way, I was glad her first time had been with me.

Still, this changed things. It had probably just made our whole situation a lot more complicated, but it couldn't be taken back now. We'd just have to deal with the consequences.

All of a sudden, everything felt different. The sex felt... meaningful. And I felt some kind of way about the cuddling, too. I couldn't quite define it, but there had been meaning in the afterglow, too. I'd wanted to hold on to her. Let her hold on to me.

It wasn't anything I'd ever felt with Claudia. Even when things had been at their best between us, when we'd found our stride as a couple a few years back, I had never felt close to Claudia the way that I felt—had always felt—close to Emzee. Because Emzee and I were friends. Or at least, that's what I had always chalked it up to.

But now everything had been cast in a new light. I realized I'd never *connected* to Claudia during sex the way I just had with Em. Never even felt the slightest impulse to cuddle, let alone actually instigate or allow it. Fucking Claudia had been hot and fulfilling, of course, and I'd certainly made sure that she'd enjoyed herself—but for us, the act had always felt more like checking a box. Meeting a need, whether physical or emotional. It hadn't felt like it really meant anything. It was just another activity we were committed to taking part in as a team.

With Emzee, though, the sex had felt different. I couldn't quite put my finger on it, couldn't really explain it, but it was new territory for me. Of that I was certain.

I splashed some cold water on my face, not sure what to do about the unwelcome and unexpected feelings that were pinballing around inside me. I hated when shit got complicated out of nowhere.

Instead of going straight back to the bedroom, I went to the kitchen. Usually, at this point in the evening, I'd be eying the door and going through a long list of possible excuses I could make as I snuck out in the middle of the night.

I took out some tea instead, which I knew Emzee liked to drink when she couldn't sleep.

Munchkin joined me. He was still wearing his leash. Em and I had been so eager to get to the bedroom that we'd been all over each other the moment we got in the apartment, with no time to even unleash the dog.

He didn't seem to mind, though, wagging up at me as I unhooked his leash and hung it on the hook next to the door. I played with his pointy ears and gave him a few scratches as I waited for the water to boil. Once our mugs of tea were ready, I spiked them with a few dashes of whisky for good measure.

Munchkin appeared to approve, wagging his tail at me before returning to his little bed in the living room, clearly sensing that Emzee and I deserved some more privacy. He was a smart, thoughtful little dog. I knew he got anxious if Em wasn't home enough, but he was never clingy when I came over to hang out, which I appreciated. Whether that spoke more highly of me or the dog, I didn't know.

I headed back to the bedroom with the tea, but when I opened the door, I found that Emzee was no longer sprawled out wantonly across the bed, but instead had slipped under the covers, hiding all her glorious soft skin and sexy-as-fuck curves.

What stopped me in my tracks was the look on Emzee's face as I walked over to her. The smile she gave me—full of pure happiness—hit me right in the gut.

Something I normally managed to keep at bay, even when I was doing the full puppet master routine on her.

If she ever found out...

Well. I'd just have to make sure she didn't.

Seeming to sense my hesitation, her smile faltered.

"Is something wrong?" she asked, biting her lip.

As she looked at me, her grip on the sheet loosened and it dipped down, revealing her absolutely perfect tits. They were full and round, almost too large for her petite frame, but oh-so perky, having that mouthwatering teardrop shape a man couldn't resist. Even though we'd just fucked, I found that I was ready to go again, my cock responding to her of its own accord.

"Yes," I said, setting the tea down on her nightstand. "There is."

My dick was rock hard as I climbed into bed beside her.

"What is it?" Emzee asked, looking adorably nervous.

I tugged the covers away, revealing the entirety of her naked body. I didn't think it was possible, but I grew even harder at the sight, my balls aching.

"I'm not inside you right now," I said. "I think we need to remedy that, don't you?"

Her eyes lit up, then widened as she got a glimpse of my cock. I knew I was well-endowed, but I'd never gotten the kind of reaction that Emzee had given me when I first revealed myself to her. Getting that same reaction now only made me want her more.

I dug around for another condom and then rolled it on, eager to take her again. Emzee seemed just as eager, her hands reaching down to stroke me as her mouth found my neck.

I didn't want to deal with my guilt now. Instead, I focused on something I could control. Making sure my fake fiancée came her brains out.

"Are you ready for me?" I asked, circling her pebbled nipple with my thumb.

She nodded, still biting her lip in a way that was both enticing and adorable.

"You want my cock inside you?" I prodded.

"Yes," she said breathily.

"Get on your hands and knees and face the headboard," I ordered her.

I loved that she immediately did as I asked, her tits

swaying heavily as she positioned herself on the bed, her heart-shaped ass directed toward me. I slid a hand down the silky smooth skin of her back before parting her thighs wider and sliding a hand between her legs.

"Fuck yes," I said. "You're more than ready."

I slipped a finger into her easily, feeling her body clench around me. I wanted to feel that around my cock.

Kneeling behind her, I gripped her hips and positioned the tip of my dick at her entrance, easing myself into her inch by inch. She moaned as I did, arching her back to accommodate my girth. She was still so fucking tight, especially from this angle, but now I knew exactly why, and I felt satisfaction in knowing that I was the only man who had ever taken her this way.

Gathering her long, silky hair into a ponytail with one hand, I pulled her head back until she gasped and then began to fuck her, knees braced on the bed, my other hand tight around her hip as I slammed into her, each thrust making my hips hit her ass with a satisfying smack.

"Fuck," she moaned, her hands fisting the sheets.

It was so hot, watching from this angle, seeing my cock spearing in and out of her. I slid my hand from her hip, down between her legs, until I found her tight, wet slit, my cock hammering into it below. She cried out as I stroked her, finding her clit and rubbing it as I fucked her from behind, harder and faster, relishing every desperate moan I drew from her.

I was close, but I wanted to feel her clench around me again.

"Get on your stomach," I told her, releasing her hair. "Facedown, and cross your legs. More friction."

She did as I asked. I lowered myself onto her and entered her again, digging my thumb into her asshole as I fucked her, making her squirm and pant like an animal.

"You like that?" I said. "You like how I'm touching you?"

"Yes," she gasped in between heaving breaths.

"I want you to touch yourself, too," I commanded. "I want you to feel my cock against your fingers while I'm fucking you."

Her hand slipped down between her legs, her hips grinding harder as she stroked her own clit, and then I felt it —felt her orgasm rush through her as she cried out into the sheets, her pussy clenching and shuddering tightly around me.

I managed only two more strokes before I climaxed too, the two of us collapsing in a heap afterward, our bodies fitting together like puzzle pieces as we drifted off to sleep.

EMZEE

CHAPTER 22

Let's be honest. I had fantasized about hooking up with Ford Malone ever since I was sixteen years old. In my mind, we'd done it in every position possible, in every possible location, giving each other an infinite number of orgasms. Mine, real. His, imagined.

But no matter how extravagant the fantasies I'd conjured about having sex with Ford were, nothing came remotely close to the reality of what had happened between us a few days ago. Whenever I thought about that night, which was admittedly far too often now, I got wet instantly. My lower belly would tighten, and I'd have to squeeze my legs together against the hot ache I felt for him. For his cock. It was hard to focus on anything other than my vivid daydreams about all the things we'd done. Especially since the pleasant soreness between my legs had lingered, making me shiver with memories of Ford every time I touched myself.

He hadn't left my place until early the next morning, though it was less a result of him falling asleep afterward than the fact that we couldn't stop banging each other until the sun came up. We'd attempted to take a shower together at one point, intending to rinse the sweat from our bodies, but had ended up fucking against the tiled walls, Ford taking me again from behind.

Soon after that he had left, hair still damp, but he had been smiling. So had I. It was still hard to believe that my first time hadn't turned into a complete and awkward disaster the way I'd always feared. There was definitely some wisdom to waiting for the right person instead of being in a rush to get it over with—at least, it had worked out well for me. I knew not everyone had the privilege of making that choice, though, and I was beyond grateful for it.

"You almost ready?" my assistant Brielle asked, bringing me back to reality.

"Yes. We're good to go," I said, resisting the urge to fan my face.

I had been standing by the equipment table for the last few minutes, completely lost in dirty thoughts. Brielle frowned, searching my face.

"Are you okay?" she asked. "You look a little pink. You're not coming down with a fever, are you? I can't get sick. I'm going on vacation next week. Can I get you a water?"

"I'm fine," I said, feeling my face get even hotter under her scrutiny. Brielle was the perfect assistant for me, usually —high energy and attentive to every last detail. But she was a lot to handle when I was off my game. "Just sweating in here, is all. Water would be great."

I had a feeling that I could dump that water over my head and it still wouldn't cool me off enough. I gave myself a mental slap and tried to refocus on the work at hand.

Today I was running a standard photo shoot at Danica Rose Management. The agency kept a studio on one of the upper floors, mostly for taking headshots of newer models or updated photos for the portfolios of more senior talent. I occasionally used the space myself, but only when I needed more controlled lighting at my disposal than what I could manage at my loft.

With a cool bottle of water deposited in my hand, I got my lenses in order and prepared to start shooting. It occurred to me that Galina might like to be on set to practice working directly with new models, and I made a mental note to invite her along next time as an official photographer's assistant so she could get some hands-on experience and punch up her resume.

The first half of the day was a complete success. We sped through our to-do list of new headshots, and I even got a few of the models to agree to come back at the end of the day for some more experimental shots I had in mind for my personal portfolio.

We were just about to break for lunch when I realized we had an audience.

It wasn't Ford this time, but the visitors were just as unexpected.

My brothers.

I waved at Stefan and Luka as they stood near the doorway, watching. They nodded, but neither of them smiled as they continued what appeared to be a very serious conversation.

My stomach churned with nerves as I tried to focus on wrapping up the current shot on my list. Even though the studio was in the office building where my brothers clocked in every day, they didn't generally poke their heads in when I was working. Yet today, they both had.

Something was up.

Had the Lunch Vault been broken? Did my brothers

know I'd lied about the true nature of my relationship with Ford? I trusted my sisters-in-law and didn't want to believe they'd spill my secrets, but I couldn't think of any other reason Stefan and Luka would come here.

"Let's break for lunch," I called out, anxiety rushing through me as the room emptied out. As soon as everyone was gone, I strode over to my brothers to confront them.

But before I could speak, Stefan said, "We need to talk." His voice was tense.

Crap. "What's up?" I asked, trying to sound neutral.

It was ironic they'd find out about my sham with Ford now, right when I was starting to think that something real was actually happening with him. The way he'd wrapped his arm around me after we'd had sex, and then brought me tea, and actually spent the night at my place...it felt like it was all adding up to something, and I prayed I wouldn't be asked to pull the plug on my fake wedding. It seemed preposterous, given that both of my brothers had had arranged marriages. Plus, I was an adult who could marry— or fake marry—whomever I wanted. Still, they *were* intensely protective. Especially when it came to me and my perceived honor.

Except that wasn't the issue at all.

"It's the Russians," Stefan said. "The threats are still coming."

Luka nodded somberly.

My heart dropped. I was relieved that my brothers didn't know what was going on between me and Ford, but in the haze of everything that had been happening, I had barely given a thought to the Bratva and the enormous ax they were holding over our heads.

Panic must have been written all over my face, because Luka was quick to jump in.

"We don't want you to worry about it," he said.

"Not worry about it?" I asked. "This affects our entire family, and our business."

"Look, Em," Stefan said. "We wanted to keep you in the loop, but at the end of the day, they aren't your problem. We are handling it. Leave everything to us."

"That's right," Luka cut in. "The whole point of this talk was that we wanted to be sure you weren't worrying yourself about it when you should be focusing on your wedding."

"I know," I said with a sigh. "I'm trying to do that."

I didn't believe the situation with the Bratva was under control—not by any means—but I knew that this was their way of taking care of me. It was touching. And even though I didn't love being shut out of the conversation, I also knew that there wasn't much I could do.

"Serious stuff aside, we also came to talk about the good stuff," Stefan said.

I raised my eyebrows. "Like what?"

"You know what," Luka said, nudging me with his elbow. "How's our baby sister feeling about approaching Married Life?"

He waggled his eyebrows, and I couldn't help but laugh.

"Aren't you excited?" Stefan asked. "Both of our marriages were arranged. We don't know anything about actual courtship. How's it all going? Spill it."

Guess it wasn't just The Wives wanting to live vicariously through me. I felt a rush of tenderness toward my brothers. It was really very sweet how concerned they were about me and Ford. Perhaps it hadn't escaped them after all, that the majority of my previous relationships had basically crashed and burned before they even really got started. I certainly had never introduced Stefan or Luka to any of my past boyfriends. They didn't tend to stick around long enough.

"Seriously, don't ask me," I said, grinning. "Ford and I have been friends for a million years. This is more like an extension of that than the whirlwind romance you seem to think it is."

It was the closest I'd gotten to telling them the truth so far, and I felt guilty for continuing to hide the fact that Ford and I had merely entered into a formal and legally binding agreement rather than an actual relationship. Especially considering that my brothers were going to be spending a lot of money on the whole charade...and that The Wives already knew what was really going on. Should I tell Stefan and Luka?

"You have to be at least a little excited about the wedding details," Luka insisted. "You have an artist's eye, after all. Did you pick out your colors or whatever?"

I laughed out loud again. "You'll have to talk to your wives about that. They're the ones planning everything, more or less. Though I am allowed to exercise a veto. And I said no pink."

Stefan gave me a grin. "I wouldn't be surprised if it was a black and white wedding, knowing you. Our own little Wednesday Addams."

"We'll see what Tori thinks about that," I said.

As they rattled on about how happy they were for me, I continued wrestling with the possibility of shattering their illusions via the very unromantic truth about my engagement.

"Ford's a great guy though," Luka was saying. "I'm glad it's gonna be him."

"Hmm?" I said, realizing I'd zoned out.

"You know we love him for you as a human and all that,

but even more so business-wise," Stefan added. "I don't think I could have chosen better if I'd chosen for you."

Both of my brothers laughed and I joined them, hoping they wouldn't pick up on how forced my chuckle was.

"But all jokes aside, seeing you happy is really the best part," Stefan said. "It's been a rough year."

"It has," I agreed, all of us sobering up as the shadow of our father's misdeeds loomed over us. "I really am happy, though."

It wasn't a complete lie.

"I'm glad," Luka said. "God knows what Dad would have had planned for you."

"He wouldn't have given me any choice," I said immediately. "In fact, I'm sure he already had someone picked out. Someone who would have benefited him and his plans."

Both of my brothers nodded, their expressions dark.

"He really fucked with all of our heads, didn't he?" Stefan mused.

It was a rare moment of honesty. None of us liked talking about how hard it had been, growing up with Konstantin Zoric as our father. Not just because he was a workaholic who was rarely home, too busy hiding his other life as a sex trafficker from us to act like an actual parent— but because we hadn't had a mother or any other close relatives to balance it all out.

Our mom had died when I was just two years old, too young to remember much of her, but my brothers had been old enough to remember her warmth and her laugh, how she'd loved painting. How much she'd truly loved us all. I wished I had even one single sweet memory to hold on to the way my brothers did.

But in the end, her love couldn't protect any of us from the monster that our father became. We never got to see how real love—and loving relationships—worked. It was amazing we had survived his controlling tyranny at all, let alone survived so well, considering how messed up we all were because of him and the long years of emotional and verbal abuse.

I knew I'd been on the receiving end of the least of it, because I was a girl, but I still bore my fair share of emotional scars from our father's behavior.

For most of my life, I'd been the odd person out. The youngest. The quietest. The only girl. When I'd gotten bullied in school, developing psychosomatic stomach pain that kept me home too many days, the nurse finally called my father at work to report my excessive absences, which he knew nothing about. He came home early that day to ream me out and I'd broken down and admitted what was really going on. He had been furious. Not at the bullies, though.

He'd been furious at me.

"How could you let this happen?" he had raged. "You're a Zoric—they should fear you, respect you. You need to show them who you are."

His advice just made me feel worse. If it hadn't been for Ford stepping in to quell the bullying, I might have never made it out of high school in one piece.

But I pushed those memories and feelings aside as I smiled up at my brothers.

"Forget him," Luka said, clapping a hand on Stefan's shoulder. "Just look at all of us now. Tori's due soon, and you're gonna be a great dad. I know it."

"And you'll be a great uncle," Stefan said. "And you, Em, are going to be the best auntie a kid ever had."

"Not to mention, Luka's going to be a great papa himself," I pointed out.

"You'll be an auntie twice over! And a beautiful bride,"

Luka said, a little bashfully. Probably due to the unusual amount of genuine sentiment we were all expressing, so unlike ourselves and so not in line with the way we'd been raised.

Our father had scarred all of us, but now that he was gone—locked away for life, behind bars—we all had a chance at a real life. Real love. A fresh start.

"We didn't ask to get born into this family," I said. "But I'm so lucky I get to have the two of you as brothers."

"I don't regret being born a Zoric," Luka said. "I just wish our dad had been anyone but Konstantin."

"He's gone now," Stefan said. "And we have to let the past go, as impossible as that sounds. All we can do now is just...try our best to move on, and rebuild better. Together."

The unspoken part, of course, was that the current mess with the Bratva was the direct result of our father's actions. But I got what Stefan was saying. He was telling us that we were in this together, that we were a family, a united front. No matter what.

In the end, I never got up the nerve to tell Stefan and Luka the truth about Ford. My brothers were so thrilled for me and my love match that I couldn't bear to burst their bubble—and after our unexpected family bonding moment, no way was I going to admit that my happy ending was a big fat lie.

At least I had already decided that I was going to be donating my monetary wedding gifts to See Yourself's mentoring program. That way, no matter what happened between Ford and me afterward, something good would come out of our wedding—farce or not.

EMZEE

CHAPTER 23

"Oooh, how about this one?" Tori squealed, whirling around with yet another voluminous monstrosity of tulle and seed pearls on a hanger.

"Oh, um, wow," I said, trying to sound not-so-horrified. "It's so...Cinderella."

Tori frowned. "Too ball-gowny?"

"Everything you love is too ball-gowny, Tor," Brooklyn said from an adjacent rack.

"She can at least give it a try," Tori pointed out, waving over one of the shop employees. "Can you please add this one to the dressing room? Thank you so much."

"Speaking of which," Brooklyn said, "I think it's time you got in there, Em."

My regular Vault Lunch with The Wives had been cancelled, my sisters-in-law having decided to forgo our usual date in favor of whisking me off to try on "dream" wedding dresses. The wedding dresses of *their* dreams, apparently. Not that I was surprised.

Michelle, Tori's stepmother, had managed to secure a

private appointment for the three of us at Blue, one of the most exclusive bridal salons in Chicago. That meant the shop was closed to everyone in the city except me, Tori, and Brooklyn, and that for the next few hours, all of the employees were at our beck and call.

My anxiety was through the roof.

Even though I knew there were no wrong choices—all the dresses were beautiful, and my sisters-in-law were nothing but sweet and encouraging—I'd approached the outing with trepidation. Regardless of the fact that the wedding was fake, the urge to find exactly the right dress was real. I'd have basically a million pairs of eyes on me during the ceremony (and after, via the tabloids and society pages), and I had to look perfect. But I still wanted to look like me.

Problem being, there wasn't a single scrap of black fabric to be found in the bridal shop.

I knew, of course, that I would be wearing a white dress. I wasn't interested in rocking the proverbial boat, especially not on my wedding day. But the act of actually showing up at Blue to try on dresses today was forcing me to acknowledge the reality of the situation.

In a matter of months, I was going to be marrying Ford Malone. In a white dress. In front of our families, our friends, and the social elite of Chicago.

And as uncomfortable as I'd be in my head and my heart all day, I couldn't stand the idea of also being uncomfortable in whichever dress I ended up having to wear for hours upon end. Nor my shoes. And what about my veil? Did people still expect brides to wear veils these days?

"Come on, Em, this is only round one," Brooklyn coaxed, wrapping her arm around my shoulders to hustle me toward the dressing room. "You're going to be doing this for hours."

"That's exactly what I'm afraid of," I said dryly.

Down the hallway, I could see a pedestal surrounded by floor-to-ceiling mirrors, which I gathered I was meant to endure each time I tried on a dress. Meanwhile, Tori had settled her lovely, very pregnant self into a comfortably overstuffed chair to wait for the fashion show, as employees flitted about with glasses of champagne and dress clips and measuring tapes. Oh, joy.

My eyes actually bugged out when I saw the dressing room that had been prepared for me. At least twenty dresses were hanging from the hooks in there, and the spacious changing room looked like it had just suffered a literal explosion of tulle, satin, and lace.

"Oh boy," I murmured, my stomach knotting with overwhelm as I tried to take it all in.

I fought the impulse to run from the store. To run from Chicago. To run from this whole mess that I'd agreed to be involved in.

"I know," Brooklyn said. "It's a lot. But we have all day. Enjoy it!"

She looked so excited that I knew there was no way I could escape.

One of the Blue employees followed me into the dressing room and immediately got to work unlacing the first dress for me. It was one that Tori had chosen, exactly the kind of frothy, princess-y, over-the-top concoction that would look great on her—but as I stood there in my underwear, I could already tell that it wasn't right for me.

I'd been told to wear undergarments that could work with a variety of dresses, so I had on a nude thong and a strapless, low-back corset bra. I'd also been advised to wear heels that were about the same height as what I'd wear for the wedding, so I had my special occasion stilettos on, though I planned to switch into flats as soon as the official ceremony was over. Still, I was teetering dangerously on those heels as I stepped into the skirt, and I had to grab onto the salesgirl's arm for support to make sure I didn't accidentally tear something expensive. Once I was situated, the hoisting began.

The salesgirl tugged the dress up over my hips and then instructed me to hold the bodice against my chest as she laced me in from the back. It took almost ten minutes to get the whole thing on and fastened, and she hadn't even laced the corset completely.

I tried to turn around, hitting the salesgirl with the enormous skirts as I did. She gamely leapt out of the way as I waddled out the door, following behind me while I propelled my poofy self down the hall. The dress made quite the rustling sound. And God, it weighed a fricking ton. The thought of spending an entire night in this thing, when I could barely move, was like a nightmare. And I hadn't even seen how it looked.

The salesgirl presented me to Tori and Brooklyn with a dramatic, "Ta-da!"

Tori let out a gasp of delight as I trudged over and got some help stepping up onto the pedestal so I could finally get a look at myself.

I had to admit, I was a vision. A vision of a giant cupcake.

"What do you think?" Tori asked, hands clasped to her chest.

All I saw in the mirror were piles of white fluff, shimmering sequins, and embroidered lace. The dress overwhelmed everything. Including me. Sure, my boobs looked great, but that was the gift of big tits and a corset. They were practically overflowing, and I had a feeling that if I bent over, or breathed in too deeply, there was a real possibility I'd spill right out of the top.

"It's very, um, prom queen-ish," Brooklyn said carefully as I turned a little to the left and then the right. "What do you think, Tori?"

"It's a *gorgeous* dress," Tori said, her eyes shining. "What do you think, Em?"

Frowning, I shook my head. I had to nip this in the bud, or else I'd be stuffing myself into these kinds of princess dresses until midnight. "It is a gorgeous dress, don't get me wrong, but I feel like I'm swimming in all this fabric. I'm just too short for these styles. I mean, look at me. I look like a...a glittery pumpkin."

Brooklyn let out a snort, and then both of us were laughing, even as Tori pouted. "Try one of mine next," Brooklyn suggested. "Pretty please? I'm dying to see one of them on you."

"Sure," I said, attempting to sound upbeat. "Coming right up."

I shuffled back to the dressing room, sighing with relief when I was unlaced from the dress. The salesgirl pulled a fresh gown off of one of the hooks and handed it to me, then left me to it. I saw right away that the dress Brooklyn had chosen would require far less help than the one I'd just stepped out of. Mainly because there was practically nothing there.

Typical Brooklyn. Being a model herself, she always loved things that were avant-garde, fashion forward, and devastatingly sexy.

Though some were rather *concerningly* sexy. Slipping out of my strapless bra, I wiggled into a dress that was borderline obscene—the upper portion was sheer, flesh-toned mesh with strategically placed strips of raw silk to cover my nipples, and the skirt was thigh-skimmingly tight all the way to the knee, where it spilled into an asymmetrical hem with a ruffle. It was stunning, and would have looked amazing on Brooklyn. On me, though...

My phone buzzed at that moment, and I dug it out of my bag to find I'd gotten a text from Ford.

How's it going? he'd asked.

It is, in fact, going, I texted back. *I feel very sorry for the employees of Blue. My sisters-in-law have them running around in circles. I myself am about ready to have a heart attack.*

"Do you need any help in there?" the Blue employee asked from outside the door.

"No," I said, dropping my phone back in my bag. "I'm coming out."

I had to take mincing little penguin steps all the way to the pedestal, thanks to how tight the skirt was, and I wondered if the side seams would survive me actually sitting down.

This time it was Brooklyn that let out a gasp of excitement.

"Oh my God, Emzee, it's fucking incredible!" she exclaimed, hopping up off her chair to come over and poke at me, trailing her hand down the shimmering skirt fabric. "I've never seen anything like it."

"It's certainly...different," Tori said, obviously trying to sound impartial.

"I think there's a bit too much side boob going on," I said, narrowing my eyes at my reflection. "And too much top and bottom boob, as well. There's no way I can wear a bra with this dress."

"That's what they make fashion tape for," Brooklyn offered. "It's double-sided and super sticky. It works."

"Mm," I said, glancing at the Blue employee, whose expression remained neutral. "The thing is, I'd rather literally *die* than have Ford's mother see a wardrobe malfunction happen if the bodice shifts and exposes a full-on nipple on my way up the aisle."

Tori shot Brooklyn an apologetic smile. "I'm sorry, but I have to agree. It's really pretty, but it's also...distracting? With Emzee's chest—no offense, Em—it's impossible not to stare at the whole boob area. And those silk shreds just make it even more of an eye magnet."

Pouting, Brooklyn let out a sigh. "Fine. I can't argue with that. I concede."

Off I minced, back to the dressing room. A different Blue salesgirl was waiting for me there, a younger woman I'd taken note of earlier thanks to the black rose tattooed on her wrist.

"Marie has to go on break, but I'm here to help," she told me. "Would you like to take another turn around the store and pick a few more dresses? It sounds like you haven't really had a chance to find one *you* like. Which is kind of the whole idea, you know?"

"Yes. My God." I nodded, letting out a breath of relief. "Thank you."

She smiled. "Don't worry. This is all par for the course. Usually it's mothers-in-law, though, and they tend to be a lot more iron-willed than your sisters here. Just try to have fun."

"I'll try," I said.

I got back into my clothes and we circled the sales floor, looking for something that spoke to me. It was a beautifully designed store, chandeliers sparkling overhead, all the dresses elegantly displayed. But that was the whole problem. There were so *many* of them.

"We also have a book with the rest of our stock. I'll grab it," the girl said, darting into a back room and then returning with a thick, well-made binder that weighed a ton.

It had to be at least two hundred pages, with wedding dresses displayed on both sides of each piece of paper. I couldn't imagine where they kept all of these dresses.

With the binder under my arm, I made my way around the store again.

Everything was breathtaking, gowns covered in sparkling crystals, embellished with handsewn lace, waterfalls of ruffles spilling down them. It was an overload of the senses. I didn't even know where to direct my eyes, since every time I'd look at one dress, I was immediately distracted by the dress next to it. I'd barely covered a quarter of the salon before I gave up.

"Not seeing anything you like?" the tattooed employee asked.

"I don't even know what I like," I confessed.

She laughed. "You wouldn't be the first," she said. "Luckily, our job is to make sure you find the perfect dress. And if today isn't the day, there's always next time. No pressure."

"Okay," I said uneasily.

She must have seen something in my expression, because she gave my arm an encouraging pat.

"I have something that might help," she said, disappearing into the back room again. But it wasn't a binder she brought out this time. It was a glass of champagne.

"Here," she said. "This usually helps take the edge off."

I took the glass gratefully and downed almost half of it immediately. Then we made one more round of the racks, and by some miracle, I actually managed to find a few dresses that looked more *me*. They were simple sheaths, nothing fussy or flouncy, and cut with the kind of universally flattering shapes that I knew would make me feel comfortable *and* beautiful.

"Good luck," the employee said, winking as she dropped me back off at the dressing room and whisked away all the reject gowns.

I stripped down to my underwear and took a deep breath.

The first dress wasn't right, but it was much better than the others I'd tried. It was sophisticated, without any sparkly embellishments or skin on display. Unfortunately, with the wide boat neck and the vertical seams down the front, it made me look kind of...

"Matronly," the salesgirl murmured when I stepped out of the dressing room. "No offense. I think it just looks too old for you."

"Totally agree," I said. "No offense taken. I appreciate your professional opinion."

I didn't even bother showing it off to my sisters. It was the second dress, though, that I knew was something special. It was the perfect combination of classic and modern, feminine but without all the frills and fuss. The moment I had it on, I knew that this was it.

The cut was simple and demure, at least from the front, where it looked similar to the dress Kate Middleton had worn on her wedding day. Long lace sleeves, narrow but plunging neckline, an A-line skirt. Instead of floral appliques on the skirt and bodice, however, my dress was free of additional decoration, and there was no nine-foot train to worry about. The fabric was a lustrous, cream-colored silk charmeuse. It somehow managed to pull off the trick of skimming my curves without exposing or overly accentuating them.

The back, however, was completely open.

It reminded me of the Prada dress, and I knew Ford would love it.

I also loved it, utterly and completely, but I knew I should try on a few more of my choices before I showed Tori and Brooklyn *The One*. I needed to know for sure that it was the dress I was going to fight for.

I'd just hung it back up behind the others and was standing there in my bra and thong, deciding which to try on next, when I heard the dressing room door creak. I turned around, expecting the salesgirl, but it wasn't an employee coming in to help me with a zipper.

It was Ford.

"What are you doing here?" I hissed.

"It sounded like you were having a rough time, so I came to offer my support." He hushed me with a smile, his eyes roving over my body. "I can't rescue you, but I can give you a little something else to think about."

I put my hand on my hips, pretending to be mad when I was actually thrilled that he was standing there. We'd spoken plenty since that night at my apartment, but had been too busy to get together.

"You know you're not supposed to see the dress before the wedding day," I scolded him.

"Then it's a good thing you aren't wearing one," he said.

With that, he swept me into his arms, his mouth coming down aggressively over mine. A little moan escaped me as I kissed him back eagerly, craving his mouth, his body. Everything. I wanted him so bad that I didn't care we were in a dressing room in a bridal shop with nothing more than a thin door and a short hallway between me and my sisters-in-law and a bunch of on-the-clock Blue employees.

Ford pushed me up against the wall, putting his finger to his mouth to indicate that I needed to be quiet. My eyes went wide as he pulled a condom out of his pocket. Never in my wildest dreams would I have imagined something like this happening. Part of me thought I should stop him, but the other part of me—the more insistent part of me—wanted to keep going.

I pushed my hips against his, feeling the long, hard press of his cock between my legs. I was basically naked already, but Ford still made a point of stripping off my bra and thong. Then he gave me the condom and started unzipping his pants.

I understood that I was supposed to help, my hands trembling a little as I tore the packet open. Even though we'd had sex before, Ford had always handled the condom. Putting it on him felt intimate in a new way, and I loved how his head fell back as I touched him.

After pushing me face-first against the wall, he used his foot to nudge my feet apart, making room for himself between my legs. His hard cock pressed against me from behind, and I was so wet for him that when he slid into me, my body was ready.

I was grateful for his hand coming up to cover my mouth, because I could barely contain the moan that slipped from my lips as he pumped deep inside of me. I was still tight, so very tight, but it felt good. And it felt even better when he began to move faster, his teeth closing gently over my shoulder, his free hand sliding around to toy with my clit.

We didn't have much time, and there was a huge chance that we'd get caught, but I didn't care. I wanted this. I wanted him. He took me hard and fast against the wall, my legs spread wide, my heels giving me just enough height to provide the perfect angle for the two of us. It was so hot, so fucking hot, both of us struggling to stay silent and discreet, me sucking the finger of the hand he still had over my mouth.

I didn't think it would be possible to come so quickly, but I could feel an orgasm racing toward me. Before I could stop myself, I was coming, clenching hard around Ford's cock, bracing myself against the wall as he shuddered with his own climax, his cock pulsing inside me.

We stayed like that for a moment, his hand muffling my cries, my knees wobbly.

Slowly he withdrew.

When I managed to turn around, his pants were zipped back up and he looked exactly as he had when he snuck in a few moments ago. It was hard to believe what had just happened, but I didn't regret it for a moment.

I slipped back into my thong and my bra and Ford gave me one last kiss before he snuck back out, neither of us saying another word. Footsteps approached from down the hall, and Tori called out, "Emzee? Everything okay in there? Do you need help?"

"No!" I said quickly. "I'm almost ready. Be out in a minute."

I caught a glimpse of myself in the mirror. My hair was coming loose, my eyeliner smudged, my cheeks flushed. I cleaned up my eye makeup with a tissue, hurried back into the dress I'd been wearing before Ford came in, and strode confidently down the hall to the pedestal.

Stepping up onto it, I smiled at my reflection. "I think this is the one," I said.

They both started clapping, and I saw tears in Tori's eyes.

"We agree," she said.

Brooklyn grinned. "There's no doubt," she said. "Look at you—you're actually glowing."

She was right. Only it wasn't because of the dress I was wearing. It was because of Ford.

EMZEE

CHAPTER 24

I had never been the kind of girl who liked to dream about my wedding day. My life goals for as long as I could remember—going way back to when I was a child—consisted of simple things, like having a house of my own with no boys allowed (which I'd more or less achieved with the loft, though my feelings about boys had definitely matured), being able to take care of myself (I liked to think I was doing pretty well in that regard), and getting a dog (hello Munchkin). I hadn't done too bad, all things considered.

The downside being that every detail relating to my upcoming nuptials had hit me like a freight train. I simply wasn't prepared for any of it. Had never deigned to consider the difference between colors called "oyster" and "feather," the religious affiliation of our officiant, the flowers that would work best for the groomsmen's boutonnieres, or the catering budget per guest. Thank God Tori and Brooklyn had managed to pull everything together with minimal input from me.

Because suddenly, Wedding Week was upon us.

I couldn't believe how fast the time had passed.

I also couldn't believe how big a shindig it had turned into. Last I'd heard, there were over six hundred people on the guest list. Did I even know six hundred people? Was this actually happening?

The reality of the situation didn't fully sink in until we got to O'Hare to catch our flight from Chicago to Ford's family's summer house on Martha's Vineyard, where we'd be holding the big event. I was nervous about basically everything as we waited to board the plane. It was making me worry about nothing, like the guy I kept catching with his eyes on me across the lounge. If he actually *was* staring at me, it was probably because I was hyperventilating.

My anxiety persisted throughout the entire flight, to the point where I could have sworn I saw that same suspicious guy from the airport standing at the end of the lane when Ford and I turned into the long driveway that wound through the landscaped grounds to his parents' house.

But no. Of course it wasn't the same guy. It couldn't be. I was just freaking out over everything because I WAS GETTING MARRIED.

Ford had been busy but supportive over the last month —in fact, he'd been the one to suggest that we fly to the summer house early to have a chance to ease into the events of the weekend. I'd immediately agreed, worried not just about my own cold feet, but his as well. We cared for each other, yes, but were we really going to go through with this?

Then again, did we even have a choice, at this point?

"Here we are," Ford said as he parked the car.

I lowered my sunglasses and looked out the window, taking it all in, my eyes going wide.

My family was wealthy. I'd grown up in a beautiful, lavishly expensive home, I'd gone to the best schools, traveled on private planes, and my closet was full of high-end designer clothes.

But Ford's family was *dripping* with money.

Their summer house wasn't some beachy cottage, but a sprawling estate. It sat right on the beach, and I could see the water sparkling behind it in the late afternoon light. The house itself was U-shaped, with east and west wings, so huge that I could have sworn I was looking at six or seven houses instead of one. The exterior was all clean white shingles, festooned with well cared for ivy that crawled artfully along the walls. I didn't think I'd ever seen a larger home. There had to be at least twenty bedrooms inside, and the sides of the property had two separate swimming pools with matching guest houses that looked to have at least two bedrooms each.

This was luxury I'd never seen before. I was completely overwhelmed.

"Ford, darling!" Ford's mother came out of the house, her arms wide open as she greeted him with a kiss on the cheek. She was dressed all in white linen, a perfect match for her perfect house, not a speck of dirt on either of them. I pasted a smile on my face and nodded.

She gave me a glancing look in return. It was far better than the outright ignoring I'd gotten during the first month or so of our engagement, but I had no desire to spend any more time with my in-laws than strictly necessary. Mr. Malone wasn't terrible, honestly, but he tended to disappear into the background whenever possible. Not that I could blame him.

"I'm so sorry, but I need to go check in with Brooklyn," I said, waving my cell phone and excusing myself.

"I'm sure Munch is fine," Ford said gently. "He loves it over there." He knew me too well.

"I know, but I'll feel better if I call," I said.

I'd been calling Brooklyn almost every hour to check in on my dog and make sure he was getting along with her greyhound, Mr. Kibbles. He and Munchkin had been friends at first sight, enjoying countless happy playdates together since Brooklyn and Luka had adopted Kibby from a local shelter last year, but I still couldn't stop fretting.

"Munchkin's great," Brooklyn said when she answered. "I just gave him his Kong with the organic peanut butter in it. He's having a blast."

"I'm sorry I keep bothering you," I said.

I had hiked up to the top of a grassy hill just above the beach. The sun was going down over the water, the clouds turning rosy and gold. It was a beautiful scene—everything about this place was beautiful—but staring at it did nothing to calm my nerves.

"It's okay," Brooklyn said. "I don't mind hearing from you, I just don't want you to worry. Munchkin's having the time of his life. You know he's always a good boy over here."

"I knew," I said, chewing on my bottom lip. "Thank you."

"We'll be there soon," Brooklyn promised. "Just hang in there. I'm sure it feels like the world is spinning out of control right now, but everything's going to be fine. Love you."

My brothers and sisters-in-law would be arriving the morning of the wedding. I was supposed to be using this time to get to know the rest of the Malone family. Something I was not especially looking forward to, though I hated to be a brat about it.

"Love you too," I said to Brooklyn, missing her and Tori and my brothers. "Bye."

That's really what it was, I realized. I was calling to

check in with my family more than I was concerned about my dog enjoying his little vacation. After all, my in-laws hadn't exactly welcomed me with open arms. It was only natural for me to be anxious.

Shoving my phone back in my pocket, I stood there looking out at the water for a while, my arms wrapped around me as the wind picked up.

"There you are," Ford said, coming up behind me. "Aren't you cold?"

He took off his jacket and draped it over my shoulders.

"Thanks," I said, pulling it close.

Things between us had been so good lately. Day by day, we'd become more comfortable with each other...in the biblical sense. I always wanted more of him.

Even now, despite my nerves, I wanted him.

God, he was gorgeous. The breeze ruffling his hair just so, the fading sunset emphasizing the chiseled planes of his face, the slope of his broad shoulders. I let out a soft little sigh.

"We should head back. Dinner's being served in a bit," he said. "You hungry?"

I smiled. I was, but not for dinner.

In fact, the last thing I wanted right now was to sit across the table from my soon-to-be in-laws so I could feel the weight of their overwhelming disappointment at my presence.

They had been a bit more friendly as of late, and of course they weren't overtly trying to end the engagement (at least, not that I was aware of), but his mother was still very not-thrilled that the wedding was happening. I knew the second I stepped inside the Malone Manse, I'd feel even more out of place—not just with his family, but in the face of their overwhelming wealth.

"I just need another minute," I said. "I'll be right in. Promise."

I expected Ford to leave me and head inside. Instead, he took my hand in his.

"Let's go for a walk," he said.

We headed down to the sand, the stretch of beach completely deserted. The benefit of owning a huge section of land on Martha's Vineyard was that you never had to worry about anybody crowding your private beach.

The Malone property took up most of the shoreline within view. They had a dock further down the beach and luxurious private cabanas and lounge chairs set up at various spots. There was even a little bar near the dock, though it was quiet and unstaffed at the moment.

The luxury all around made me a bit speechless.

But Ford's presence helped. Feeling his hand wrapped around mine did a lot to calm me.

"It's incredible here," I said.

"Yeah," Ford said. "It's not too shabby."

I gave him a gentle sock in the arm. It was moments like these that made me feel like something more was happening between us. It was getting harder and harder to ignore.

I shivered again, and this time Ford stopped and turned toward me. "Let's go back."

"Not yet. I'm okay," I said.

Ford lifted an eyebrow. "I could warm you up."

His voice had gone low and husky. I knew what that tone meant.

"You think so?" I asked, playing innocent.

"I guarantee it," he said, grabbing my hips and pulling me against him. I loved it when he was a little rough. And I loved that he was already hard and ready for me.

"Hmm...maybe I am getting warm," I whispered, wrapping my arms around his neck.

He bent his head down to kiss me, his tongue thrusting hard and deep into my mouth—a preview of what he was capable of giving me. I kissed him back, moaning my pleasure.

"How about now?" he asked, his hands going lower until they found the hem of my dress.

"A little warmer," I said coyly.

"Just a little?" he asked, biting the side of my neck, making me gasp.

His hands moved up until his fingers found the crotch of my panties, already soaking wet.

"Look at that," he said, sucking in a breath. "I think you're more than warm now."

He dragged his fingers back and forth, stroking me through my underwear. The extra friction made me shiver, but not from the cold this time.

Ford slid his jacket off my shoulders, releasing me long enough to lay it on the sand. Then he pulled me down onto it, positioning himself over me, pressing his body against mine.

He kissed me the entire time, his tongue tangling with mine, pulling my dress up past my hips. I'd never had sex in a public place, right out in the open (our quickie at Blue had been behind a locked dressing room door, after all), but I realized that I liked the idea.

Clearly, so did Ford. The thrill of it all turned me on, and the thought that we could get caught was beyond hot. Even though night was falling around us, I wasn't cold anymore. Not with Ford all over me, tugging my panties aside so he could thrust his fingers inside me.

I cried out with pleasure as he teased my clit with his

thumb, letting me ride his fingers at my own pace, bringing me to the edge of an orgasm before pulling his hand back.

"I'm not gonna let you come on my fingers," he growled, nibbling my earlobe. "I want to feel that tight little pussy coming around my cock."

Then he pulled out a condom, ripping it open as I worked his belt open and pushed his pants down.

"Tell me what you want," he ordered, rolling the latex down his long, hard length.

"You," I said, breathless with need.

"Tell me," he said again. "What do you want?"

I swallowed. I knew what he wanted to hear. I'd never been much of a dirty talker, but I liked when Ford did it. He loved to tell me all the explicit, nasty things he wanted to do with me—to me. And he loved narrating when we were in the midst of fucking. Now it was my turn.

"I want your big, hard cock," I said. My voice low and throaty with desire.

"What do you want me to do with it?" Ford demanded.

My knees were up, my thighs open, and I could feel the cool, salty sea air between my legs. I was so ready for him.

"Fuck me. Fuck my pussy," I said.

"Your tight, hot pussy," he prompted.

"Fuck my tight, hot pussy," I moaned.

"Good girl," Ford said with a smirk. "Spread your legs for me."

I did. I spread them wide, baring myself to him, wet and ready and waiting, and we both let out a groan as he slid home.

"Yes," I panted. "Fuck me, Ford."

He did as I asked, in slow, long strokes that made me go out of my mind, squirming in the sand, hungry for more. I closed my eyes and pressed my head back, not caring that sand was getting everywhere. Not caring that I'd probably still be washing it out of numerous unmentionable spots for the next several days.

All I cared about was Ford and his body and the pleasure he was giving me.

Then, without warning, he grabbed my knees, spreading me even wider and pressing my thighs back against my chest. I felt the difference immediately, the way his dick pumped even deeper inside me.

"Yes," I moaned, stretching out the word. "Yes, God, yes."

"Fuck," he groaned. "That's it."

I gasped at how good he felt. How close I felt to him as he started to lose control, his thrusts speeding up, his breaths hitching. I could tell he was getting close, and I was too.

Suddenly, all I wanted was to come with him. To feel that moment of release together, to be even more connected. I pulled his mouth down over mine, sucking his tongue, meeting each of his thrusts with a jerk of my hips, the two of us losing ourselves in the hot slide of our bodies.

I didn't care about the wind or the sand, didn't care that I was moaning louder and louder now, my cries probably strong enough to reach the Malone family house where his parents were likely gathered around the dinner table eating from the world's most expensive china.

I didn't care if they heard. In fact, I wanted them to.

"Emzee, fuck, Em," Ford gasped, pulling back to gaze down at me, and I knew this was it. He was coming. And so was I. Cresting the wave, my body pulsed with waves of hot pleasure, my pussy contracting hard and fast just as Ford let out a roar, finding his own release.

We lay there in the sand after, both of us breathing

heavily, the night air cooling our hot bodies as the sounds of the waves surrounded us.

For the first time since all of this had begun, I allowed myself to believe in the happy ending that The Wives had been spinning. Could this really work between me and Ford?

I was finally starting to believe that maybe—just maybe —it would.

FORD

CHAPTER 25

I'd always loved spending summers on Martha's Vineyard when I was a boy. It was an escape from the noisy hustle of the city and the intensity of my family's busy daily life. When we were here, my parents could avoid each other easily; my father spending all day at the club golfing, my mother by the pool with an ever-present cocktail and a gaggle of lady friends. With each of us off on our own, we could find a sense of peace that was impossible to achieve in Chicago. Left to my own devices, I'd spend all day at the beach, collecting shells and swimming.

The stretch of sand on our property had long ago become my happy place.

Last night, it was my happy place for a completely different reason.

Claudia would have never allowed me to fuck her on the beach. She would have whined about getting sandy or messing up her hair or being too cold or whatever.

Emzee was everything that Claudia wasn't.

At the moment, Em was sleeping soundly next to me in the bed we would share until the wedding was over and we left for our honeymoon. She'd been fucked hard and good and to the point of sheer exhaustion. Just like she deserved to be.

We'd snuck back to the house later than we intended, having missed dinner with my parents. While Emzee showered off all the sand that had managed to burrow into the various crevices of her body, I apologized for our absence, explaining that Em had a migraine coming on and that I'd put her to bed early. My mother was surprisingly understanding, probably because she herself was a migraine sufferer, and my father—per usual—didn't seem to care either way.

Our housekeeper, Mrs. Windham, was more than happy to put together a tray of leftovers for me to bring up to the bedroom. She stayed on at the Vineyard property year-round, managing the landscaping and the utility bills and the general upkeep of the house, but she also adored me and had spoiled me rotten since I was a child. The picnic she foisted on me consisted of creamy parmesan polenta, grilled lemon asparagus and shrimp, a green salad with oil and vinegar, and half a bottle of wine. Mrs. Windham had also added a silver pot of hot cocoa with a dish of mini marshmallows on the side. She'd always brought me hot cocoa before bed when I was a child. Apparently, me being twenty-three and a full grown adult hadn't changed her view of me at all.

Emzee and I had eaten everything out on the balcony, wrapped up in our robes, and then promptly engaged in another round of strenuous intercourse before passing out in bed together.

Now, staring down at her, I felt a jolt in my chest at the thought of our upcoming wedding. At the thought of making this thing with Emzee official. Not just official for the sake of the charade, but *actually* official.

Because something had changed. I was realizing that this might be real.

Whatever we had going on between us...our relationship felt different than it ever had before. Somewhere along the way, our game of pretend had stopped being pretend.

Emzee stirred, let out a sigh, and then turned over. I looked down at her again, feeling a strange sense of comfort. This whole thing had started so innocently. I'd needed to get my parents off my back about marrying Claudia, and Emzee had conveniently been there for me. The way she'd always been there for me. It had been a no-brainer to rope her into my scheme. Even though she had initially resisted, I'd known that she would eventually agree.

And even though I knew I was being manipulative with her, I'd never had a single doubt about my own feelings—or lack thereof. After all, my dynamic with Emzee had been set years ago, when we were teenagers, when the hero worship had begun. My justification for leaning on her all that time was that we were friends. Sure, it was unfortunate that she had a crush on me, but I'd always figured that she'd eventually get over it. That I wasn't using her so much as enjoying the advantages of our friendship. Something that I assumed was mutually beneficial.

During the last few months, though, the balance of power had started to shift. It wasn't just me relying on Emzee to constantly be my yes-person and my enabler, but the two of us relying on each other. I'd found myself craving her company, as well as her body. Her sense of humor was exactly the antidote I needed on my most stressful days, and she became the person I turned to the most, from the moment we woke up in the morning and had coffee together to the last kisses we shared at night. She was my support system, yes, but I had also become hers.

Was it sleeping with her that had done it? The power that came from being the first person to introduce her to sex, slowly but surely figuring out exactly what she liked, and showing her—training her—to give me exactly what I liked in return?

Was it getting to know her more intimately as a person, in all the ways a man would know his fiancée, rather than simply carrying on as I always had in the past by treating her as an audience for my own performances?

Maybe it was the memories we'd built, made up of inside jokes, private and professional and family dinners, enjoying—or sometimes suffering through—social engagements, the sleepless nights fueled by sex and snuggles, followed by pancake breakfasts the next morning.

Maybe it was all of it.

Maybe this was what a relationship really *was*.

My parents had never been much of a positive example of what a relationship should look like, and I had to admit that in retrospect, the relationship I'd had with Claudia for all those years had felt more fake, more like an arrangement of mutual convenience, than the agreement I now had with Emzee. The thought was jarring, but not unwelcome.

With the wedding right on our doorstep, it seemed like a good idea to go into the union with full disclosure. Well, almost full, anyway. I might leave a few details out—not to cover my ass, but to protect Emzee's feelings. She didn't need to know what an asshole I'd been about the whole thing in the beginning. The last thing I wanted to do was hurt her in any way. She deserved better. No, that wasn't right—she deserved the best.

I looked over at her again, tangled in the sheets, her bare

skin like a pearl in the light of the moon. It was hard not to reach out and touch her, rouse her into another quick fuck. Just looking at her made me hard. I imagined those lips against mine, trailing down my torso, wrapping around my cock. There was still so much to teach her, so much she could learn about pleasure—both giving and receiving. I couldn't wait to continue our lessons, especially since she was such an eager pupil. Eager and enthusiastic. Like on the beach, the way those filthy words came out of her innocent little mouth, making me so hot I almost came then and there.

What would it be like, to actually be in love with the woman I married? Was I falling in love with Emzee?

When I woke up the next morning, Emzee's side of the bed was already cold. I listened for the sound of the shower, but all was quiet. She must have gone out. I knew that she liked to start her days early.

Getting up, I pulled on a T-shirt, determined to find her and tell her the truth.

That this thing between us? It wasn't what I'd thought it was at all.

EMZEE

CHAPTER 26

I opened my eyes just as the sun was beginning to appear on the horizon. The Malone family summer home was truly gorgeous, and the view of the ocean beyond Ford's balcony was breathtaking. Part of me wanted to rustle him out of bed so we could watch the sunrise together, but when I looked over at him, sleeping soundly, he seemed so peaceful that I didn't want to wake him up.

Instead, I got up and stretched, my body feeling deliciously sore. Last night on the beach, and then again after our little room service meal, had been...well. Every part of me felt alive. As the room began to lighten, I realized that nothing would make me happier than to see the morning coming on, all by myself, before anyone else in the house was up. So I dug my sneakers out of my suitcase, threw on leggings and a Lululemon top, and headed out. As I snuck through the still-quiet house, down to the beach, I relished the peace and calm.

It was cool out, but the ocean breeze felt good against my skin, and I knew I'd warm up soon enough. I jogged along the shoreline, going at an easy pace, taking deep breaths of salty sea air and feeling the blood pumping through my veins. Who knew I'd be so into exercise in the right environment? It was the perfect opportunity to sort through all my thoughts and feelings before the wedding.

I still couldn't believe that the big day was almost here. By this time tomorrow, I would be Mrs. Ford Malone. It would be official.

But what would it mean?

I had resisted fully acknowledging the bond developing between me and my fake fiancé over the past few months, worried that my hopeful heart was making me see things that weren't there, that I was letting myself fall victim to wishful thinking.

But I couldn't deny it anymore. I wasn't making up our connection. I wasn't making up the way he'd hold me close after sex, the way he took the time to make my eggs exactly right in the morning—over medium, with just a little bit of runny yolk to dip my toast in—or the way he turned to me first when he got stressed about work or had some good news to share. We genuinely enjoyed our time together, and we relied on each other. I wasn't the sidekick anymore.

We'd always had our friendship, and now we had an intense physical connection as well. Yet I was sure our relationship was more than just the combination of those two things. And wasn't that what romantic relationships were all about, after all? Friendship and sexual attraction, plus mutual support and respect, and the desire to be with each other, in all the ways?

It seemed like ever since I gave my virginity to Ford, which was something I continued to keep a secret from him, our dynamic had shifted. At first I had assumed that the intimacy of our bodies was creating a false sense of emotional intimacy as well, but I didn't think that was the case anymore. I felt safe with him. I trusted him. It felt like we were truly growing closer—that we were becoming more and more like a real couple, day by day.

Ford and I really were kind of perfect together. I knew I wasn't wrong.

I stopped to catch my breath after a mile or so, panting as sweat rolled down my back.

The sun had risen fully, casting soft golden light all across the beach. It felt like a message, almost, an omen that I was embarking on something completely new. Something honest. Something true. I was so convinced of it that I decided I had to talk to Ford right away, before we both got swept up in the all-day festivities for the wedding. We'd probably barely see each other until I walked down the aisle toward him on my brother's arm.

I would tell him exactly how I felt. See if he felt the same. If he was willing to pledge to make this marriage a real one.

Even though I'd already built up quite a sweat coming down the beach one way, I broke that record on my return to the house. I couldn't run back to my fiancé fast enough.

The Malone family's staff was just starting to begin their morning routine when I burst through the door. I'd passed land-scapers outside, trimming the plants and bushes, tending to the leaves that had fallen into the pools, preparing for the arrival of the guests. Huge box trucks full of tables and chairs for the wedding had pulled into the driveway as well, and workers were milling around, unloading tablecloths and heating lamps and dozens of other things whose purpose I didn't quite know.

Once again, I was beyond grateful that my sisters-in-law had taken charge. The last thing I needed was to worry about the wedding and all the little details required today.

I squeezed by the staff and headed for the stairs, my attention totally focused on getting to Ford. This conversation couldn't wait. I'd just put my foot on the bottom step when a voice stopped me.

"Oh, Mara, there you are," Mrs. Malone's voice called out from behind me. "How opportune. We need to speak with you for a moment."

Slowly, I turned around to find Ford's mother standing in the doorway of the summer house's library, her lips pressed together in a hard line. Behind her, I could see Ford's father sitting at his desk, his expression unreadable to me. Nothing about this was comforting.

"A moment," she repeated, beckoning me into the library.

"I, um, was just going to take a shower," I said, gesturing toward my sweaty appearance.

I knew Mrs. Malone hated any display of imperfection and I was the poster child for that right now. But she seemed far more concerned with us having this little chat.

"The shower can wait," she said, standing aside.

Nodding, I headed into the room, feeling like I had no choice in the matter. My pulse was pounding. But it wasn't from the run anymore.

My nervousness only increased when Mrs. Malone closed the library doors behind me, closing me in with her and her husband.

I'd barely spoken to Ford's parents since he'd dropped the engagement bomb on them. We'd seen each other socially, of course, and both of them had been polite—taking care not to snub me in any overt way that might draw attention—but even at the surprise engagement party and since Ford and I had arrived on the Vineyard, his parents and I had been keeping our distance, as if we'd made some silent agreement.

Ford had repeatedly reassured me that it was just how his parents were, with everyone, but I knew it was me personally that they didn't approve of. They'd always been warm toward Claudia, and I knew they would prefer that Ford break off our engagement and get back together with his ex. She certainly seemed like a more appropriate choice on paper.

Still, I'd hoped that maybe they'd warmed up to me, had accepted that Ford and I were going through with the wedding. His mother, at least, had stopped fighting with him about it and had redirected her energy to helping my sisters-in-law with the wedding plans. And now this.

Standing there in the library, anticipating their possible disappointment, I understood why Ford would rather fake an engagement than confront them about what he really wanted.

They were certainly formidable, and they hadn't even said a word yet.

"Please sit," Ford's father said. It was a command, not a request, and I obeyed.

Mrs. Malone moved to stand beside her husband, and they both looked at me as she said, "We wanted to inform you that we are still very much opposed to this union."

Any last, lingering hope I'd had about their acceptance crumbled into dust.

"I'm sorry to hear that," I said, glad that my voice didn't shake. "But we are still getting married. Were you... expecting us to break it off?"

Ford's mother smirked at me. "Don't be ridiculous," she said. "Calling off the wedding now would be too loud, too much fodder for the gossip columnists."

I relaxed a little. Even if they didn't approve of me now, surely after Ford and I were married, they'd see how happy we were together. How much we truly cared for one another. Maybe after some time had passed, they might be able to consider me part of the family.

But that hope quickly died when Ford's mother went on.

"That being said, of course we can't allow this to go on forever," she said. "It's an utterly unacceptable match. So. You have one year to get this reckless, foolhardy 'love' out of your system, and then you and Ford will be done."

I stared at her. Her plan sounded suspiciously close to the one that Ford and I had agreed upon, but I knew his parents had no idea that this whole arrangement had been strictly that—an arrangement. It just sounded so distasteful and sordid coming from her mouth. As if it was preposterous to think the two of us could possibly have real, enduring feelings for each other.

"What if we don't want to be done?" I asked, managing to find my tongue.

"Please," Mrs. Malone said with a sneer. "Your shine will have worn off by then. Besides, we can spin this any way we like when reports of your affair start getting leaked to the press."

My jaw dropped, my stomach clenching at the implication. "My affair?!"

I would never cheat on Ford. That was absolutely insane.

Ford's mother crossed her skinny arms over her surgically enhanced chest. "Believe us," she said, "if you aren't willing to walk away, we'll make sure that your name is tarnished forever. Can your family really afford another scandal, after everything your father did?"

"This is really...really..." I trailed off, at a loss for words. I couldn't believe what I was hearing. My eyes darted over to Ford's father, hoping that he was just as shocked by his wife's words as I was, but he barely seemed to care that a conversation was happening in the first place. He had his nose buried in the *Wall Street Journal*. Clearly, he was going to let his wife do whatever she wanted.

I felt sick. Was my whole life going to just be one humiliation after another?

Ford's mother seemed to be enjoying my speechlessness, and even came over to give me a little condescending pat on the arm. I was so stunned that I couldn't even move.

"Now, now," she cooed with faux sympathy. "We realize this won't be easy for you, so we'll be sure to take good care of you when you go."

I stared at her, feeling numb. But she wasn't done.

"A little Russian bird tells us that your family left a few unsettled debts unpaid when the agency changed hands. We can take care of that for you. And just like that, all your problems are solved. Of course, if you should screw this up in any way..."

How had Ford's family found out about the Bratva and the debt they were holding over our heads? Stefan and Luka had said they had the situation under control, but if the Malones knew about it, maybe it was more precarious than we had originally thought.

I swallowed hard.

I wanted to argue. To fight for what I knew I had with Ford.

But I fully understood the threat Mrs. Malone had just laid out. The offer she'd made to help my family get rid of the Russians. My brothers said they'd handle it, but how could they? They simply didn't have access to the kinds of funds that the Bratva was after. And even if they did, there was no guarantee that the Bratva wouldn't just come back six months or a year after they'd received their payment to demand more.

On the other hand, Ford's parents were obviously in tight with the mob. That was the only way they could have known about the Bratva's threats. They also had more money than I could wrap my head around. Could they really fix this? Make it all go away for good?

I glanced over at Ford's dad. He had lowered his newspaper and was looking at me with a searching expression. I didn't see judgment there, I saw...assessment. As if he was waiting to see if I'd make the smart move.

There was no denying what was at stake. It wasn't just about me—it was about my whole family. Their safety and security, their ability to continue forward with the business and their livelihoods. Stefan and Luka had wives to care for, babies on the way...

If I agreed to let the Malones clear this debt, the sins of my father could finally be washed away.

"Once the debt is paid, we'll be done with them forever?" I asked.

"Forever," Ford's mother promised. "But only if you walk away after a year."

I could feel my heart shattering, knowing that I was going to have to choose between my family and Ford. But it was no choice at all.

"Fine," I said. "You have a deal."

I'd stick to the original plan. A year of marriage with Ford, and then I'd say goodbye.

I'd never seen my mother-in-law look so happy. If she smiled any more broadly, she'd probably ruin her Botox.

"You've made the right decision," she said. Then she waved her hand, indicating that I was dismissed.

Beyond devastated, I left the library.

Less than fifteen minutes ago, I'd felt like I was on top of the world. Like a new chapter in my life was about to begin —a chapter I'd be sharing with Ford.

Now, I knew that my happiness had an expiration date. One year from today.

Instead of going to find Ford, I went to another room in the house to hide. I didn't want anyone to see what a wreck I was. A bride shouldn't be so sad right before her wedding, after all.

EMZEE

CHAPTER 27

"**Y**ou look perfect," my sisters-in-law cooed.

I looked in the mirror and tried to see the beautiful, blushing bride behind the thinly veiled unhappiness I saw in my reflection.

My head ached. It was half due to the stress of that morning, and half due to the elaborate hairstyle now constructed on the top of my head with about five thousand bobby pins pinching my scalp in order to keep it in place. Soft tendrils fell down my back, so it was the best of both worlds; Ford could touch my hair all he wanted, and my updo would still look sophisticated.

But inside, I was dying.

I knew Tori and Brooklyn were doing their best to make this the most magical day of my life, and I couldn't bear to break their hearts by telling them definitively that this whole arrangement was definitely going to be ending in a year.

Still, the hair and makeup artists they had hired had done amazing work. I *did* look perfect, even though I felt terrible. My request to rock my signature winged eyeliner had been honored, my cheeks glowed with just a hint of rosy pink, my lashes were thick, and my lips were subtly glossed. Even my eyebrows were a fucking work of art. All that was left to do was put my dress on. It was hanging behind the door, still in its garment bag, another reminder of the bond that had formed between me and my fiancé.

I couldn't look at that dress without thinking about how he had snuck into the bridal salon so the two of us could have a quickie in the dressing room, the Blue employees and my sisters-in-law just a few feet away down the hall. It had been wonderful and hot and unexpected.

Exactly like Ford.

I felt tears building up, a tightening in my throat, but I knew the last thing I could do right now was cry. I couldn't ruin my makeup and I couldn't let my sisters-in-law think that anything was wrong. No one could know about the deal I had made with my in-laws.

I'd thought briefly about telling my brothers, asking for their advice, but I quickly squashed that idea. I knew what they would say. They'd tell me to follow my heart and reject what the Malones were offering—that the Zoric family took care of its own, exhibiting exactly the kind of Eastern European machismo they'd been raised to embody, for better or worse.

But the truth was, we desperately needed the Malones to bail us out. They were the only people who could square our debts, protect us from the Bratva's threats and violence, prevent our family's reputation from plummeting again, and keep Danica Rose Management from going out of business. With wives and families to support, my brothers needed DRM to be a success. I couldn't sit by and let the Bratva destroy the legacy my brothers had worked so hard to rebuild.

"Is everything okay?" Tori asked, leaning down to look at me in the mirror. "You're stressing. I can tell by that tiny little line you get between your brows."

"I'm great," I said, forcing a smile. "Just nerves."

"We get it," Tori said. "But the day's going to pass by so fast, you'll barely have time to be nervous once everything starts. I promise."

"Tori's right," Brooklyn said. "It really does go by in the blink of an eye."

Both she and Brooklyn looked absolutely gorgeous in their matron-of-honor dresses. I hadn't been able to choose between the two of them, so I had given them the title jointly, which had thrilled them. As had my request that they pick their own dresses. All I'd asked was that they go bold, nothing too pale or muted or neutral. I'd wanted to be surrounded by bright, happy colors on my wedding day.

They had each chosen something that suited them perfectly.

Tori was in a romantic, full-skirted blue floral gown by Marchesa that showed off her gorgeously rounded stomach. As always, she gave off a bit of a princess vibe, with a pair of cute matching shoes and her hair cascading down her back, perfectly curled.

Brooklyn looked every part the badass in a dramatic navy dress with gathered sleeves that was the ideal combination of sexy and wedding-appropriate. She too was showing off her baby bump, though hers was smaller than Tori's, and she'd put on a pair of colorful paisley print Dolce & Gabbana stilettos which made her look even more high-fashion.

God, I wanted so badly to confess to them what had happened with Ford's parents, but this was the kind of secret that even the Vault couldn't contain. They'd want to run directly to my brothers and have them fix this for me, and I couldn't let that happen. Besides, explaining the leverage the Malones had over our family would mean betraying my brothers, who didn't want Tori or Brooklyn to know about the threat the Bratva was holding over our heads.

On top of all that, the last thing I wanted to do was ruin the wedding my sisters-in-law had spent so much time and effort planning for me. I was grateful for their help, grateful that they were here with me. I was lucky to call them my family. We had each other. That was what I should be focusing on, not my sadness over the eventual demise of my relationship with Ford.

Besides, I'd originally entered into this arrangement knowing that it would have to end. Knowing that there was an expiration date. This was simply a shift back to Plan A. No big deal.

My eyes started to sting again.

"You ready to put on the dress?" Brooklyn asked gently.

Clearing my throat, I said, "Could you two give me a moment, actually? I think I just need to...reflect. Compose myself. Before I finish getting ready."

"Of course," Brooklyn said, giving me a wink. "It's a lot to take in, I know."

They quickly cleared out of the dressing room, gathering their stuff as they went.

"Let us know when you're ready for us!" Tori said, closing the door behind her.

And then I was alone.

I looked in the mirror again, at the girl who was about to be a bride, and took a deep breath. Today was both exactly what I'd once dreamed of having with Ford, and yet nothing at all like it at the same time. The girl in the mirror looked so pretty, so happy. Her life was simple. She was going to marry the man she loved.

The reality was a lot more complicated.

I dug a few bobby pins out of my hair, hoping it wouldn't cause the whole updo to collapse, and sat there in my robe, feeling sorry for myself.

There was a knock and I fixed the smile back on my face as I heard the door open. Apparently, Tori and Brooklyn had decided I'd had enough time to myself.

But when I turned to greet them, I found Ford standing in the doorway instead.

Of course.

He practically took my breath away in his wedding suit. It wasn't as if I hadn't seen him in a tux before—he'd worn one to the gala where he first announced our fake engagement—but this was different. Everything was different.

"Hi," he said.

"Hi," I said, dropping my gaze.

When I looked up again, he was grinning at me. I was glad I was sitting down because I was definitely swooning at the sight of him, all dressed up for our wedding day, smiling at me like I was the most beautiful thing he'd ever seen.

"You know you're not supposed to see the bride before the ceremony," I chided him.

I wasn't mad, though. In fact, I'd sort of been expecting him. That was another thing I'd always found charming about Ford: his childlike inability to follow the rules. I had known he wouldn't be able to resist sneaking in to see me before we met at the altar. It was half the reason my dress was still zipped up in the garment bag.

I turned back to the mirror, pretending to fuss with my hair as Ford came up behind me. He leaned down, wrapping his arms around my shoulders and nuzzling my ear. I admired the other us, the us I saw in our reflection. The way I wished things really were. A happy bride and her handsome husband-to-be. How desperately I wanted our mirror life to be our real life.

Ford pulled back and met my eyes in the mirror, searching my gaze. "Em."

"What?" I asked.

"Do you...love me?" he asked softly.

For a moment, I was speechless.

If he had asked me even a single day ago, my answer would have been a resounding yes. I wouldn't have had to even think about it. I'd have told him exactly what I had realized while running on the beach at sunrise—that I thought what we had between us was real, and that I wanted our marriage to be real as well.

But I was wiser now. Wiser than I'd been even a month ago. Hell, a day ago.

I'd learned my lesson. There would be no fairy tale ending for me.

Besides, there was no way I could tell Ford that I loved him knowing I was now using him, using his parents' money, exactly as brazenly as he was using me.

Because as much as I wanted to believe that things had changed between us, the fact of this very moment—of him sneaking in to see me before the wedding—only confirmed what I should have known all along. That Ford was never going to change.

He was always going to do exactly what he wanted, not what other people wanted him to do. This whole fake engagement had been his idea to begin with, and it seemed foolish now to think that it could have ever become something more. That the dynamic between us could suddenly be different than it ever had been.

Ford was always going to see me as the [...] outcast from high school who worshipped [...] walked on and would do whatever he asked. [...] me as an equal. He'd never see me as a real p[...]

It was better to accept that fact now.

"Do you?" he whispered again.

I turned and looked him straight in the eye, giving him the only possible answer I could.

"I...don't."

Emzee and Ford's story continues...

Find out what happens in The Act.

Want to be up-to-date with all my releases? Sign up for my newsletter!

ABOUT THE AUTHOR

Stella Gray is an emerging author of contemporary romance. When she is not writing, Stella loves to read, hike, knit and cuddle with her greyhound.

Made in the USA
Monee, IL
02 November 2021

81249885R00148